Dirty Little Murders

Loren Zahn

To order additional copies of this book, contact:
Xlibris Corporation
1-888-795-4274
www.Xlibris.com
Orders@Xlibris.com
55424

ACKNOWLEDGEMENTS

This book would not be possible if it were not for the wonderful circle of family and friends who helped with everything from character development to research on medical and criminal forensics. Your enthusiasm and support – your optimism and trust – your unwavering belief in this project – and me – kept me going and saw me through to the end.

PROLOGUE

She was limp in his arms. Her head lolled back exposing the long white throat; even at its awkward broken angle, it tempted him. The desire to run his tongue along the curve of it right down to the space between her breasts seized him, and for a moment, he imagined that final act could summon back her life.

Losing the closest thing to love he had ever known was regrettable, yet he considered love – unlike death – as tenuous. As he held her now in the grip that was his alone, he was aroused. Through death, he had conquered her lying and betrayal. It was an act of purification, and it freed her in a way that forgiveness never could. Like this, they were linked in the pain and inexplicable thrill of death's final moment.

"You'll always belong to me," he whispered in her ear.

He leaned slightly further, cradling her in sync with the boat's rocking. Her toes pointing downward – a ballerina poised in final pirouette.

Then, without ceremony, he let her slip.

Stella Morris's feet cut the water, and the black ocean opened its mouth to swallow her whole.

CHAPTER 1

Theodosia Hunter was sure she was dreaming – a plot or subplot forming complete with sound effects – only, the synthesized *Brandenburg Concerto* playing out was real. It was her cell phone and its insistent ringing at 3:00 a.m. meant trouble. She had been in that murky place between dozing and waking up when it went off. That's the way it started.

"Hullo?" The word was a struggle, coming out dull and thick.

"Theo, it's Frank."

Not too long ago, Frank Marino's voice was the one she heard paired with gentle neck nuzzling and comforting closeness. Now, with their angry breakup still a fresh gash in her heart, hearing it now, over the phone, was all wrong.

"Uh-huh?"

She mumbled, apprehension prickling her neck; she was aware that her stomach started to knot up.

He was quick and to the point.

"Theo, I think we've found Stella." His voice softened, "But it's not good."

She sucked in her breath. It was loud enough for Frank to hear through the phone. Now, she was awake; the dullness of sleep completely shattered. Her voice came too quickly and grated in her own ears.

"Where is she? What happened?"

There was no other way to say it so Frank just said it the way a veteran cop would.

"The border patrol was doing a sweep for illegals in the Tijuana Slough and found a woman, looks like she drowned. The dead woman *could* be Stella."

Theo was still trying to connect a body found in the swampy border area with her friend who'd been missing only a few days. It was a puzzle she couldn't logically piece together.

"Stella wouldn't go near Tijuana. She was afraid of the border area. It can't be her."

It seemed like a logical conclusion and one that subtracted Stella from the ugly equation.

Frank expected her reaction. It was the kind of denial that usually followed after an announcement of bad news, and he had lots of experience in getting past it when dealing with a victim's family or friends. Only this was different. This was Theo. He couldn't bear the thought of handling her by the book like he was supposed to. He took a deep breath and began to gently maneuver her out from behind the rock of denial.

"I don't think it has anything to do with being *in* Tijuana, Theo. The body was probably washed into the slough from the ocean. It happens all the time. It's the currents. This body seems to have been in the water for a while. We're guessing it was a swimming accident. She could have gotten caught up in a rip current. Those can easily overwhelm even the strongest swimmer. We won't really know until we perform an autopsy. Right now, with no clothing or identification, it'll take us longer to make a positive ID."

"No clothing?"

Theo said, queasiness twisting that stomach-knot.

"Well, that's not unusual." Frank continued. "Lots of forces come into play when a body is in ocean for awhile." He said this under his breath and just a little too fast. Theo picked up on it. She was immediately alert to something else, something he wasn't telling her. She was all business now – the reporter looking for clues. Theo cleared her throat and started in.

"What was the damage, Frank?"

He had hoped to avoid going into a detailed description of what happens to a body caught in swells and pulled out to sea. The ones that aren't suspended in the local currents are never found. But when the body is caught in the offshore tides, it gets agitated around like rags in a washing machine where fish and sea mammals may feed on it until it's pulled closer in to shore. Once trapped in the local stream, it would be battered against coastal rocks until an undertow funneled it into the marshy no-man's land at the southwest corner of San Diego County that separates the United States from Mexico – the Tijuana Slough. Although he didn't say any of this, he knew Theo's shrewd mind was processing what was implied.

"There's a starting point in any identification process." He began, avoiding a direct response. "This will just help us eliminate other possibilities."

Frank thought the explanation rolled off his tongue weak and officious – a department bureaucrat trying to finagle a union of minds for his own purpose;

he hoped she didn't hear it. The silence on Theo's end snuffed that hope like grinding out a cigarette – something Frank wished he'd had right then.

The pause stretched. He could sense the eyebrow lift over the phone as clear as if she were standing in front of him, glaring.

"Shit!" Frank mouthed the word silently, mentally kicking himself. He figured he had just slid out on thin ice. He didn't want to wait for Theo to start battering him with pointed questions. He tried an offensive maneuver.

"I'm sorry, Theo, I can only imagine how tough this must be for you. But, and I know *you* know this is so, we need to start someplace . . . I was hoping you could help us. We . . . *I* . . . really need your help."

Her silence made him wonder if they'd lost the connection. "Theo?" he asked softly.

It was but a momentary break. He'd soon miss the shelter of that brief respite.

"You can't identify her!"

It was not a question. Frank couldn't tell if it was a stunned response or a piercing accusation. Suddenly, he was conscious of the hairs on the back of his neck. He figured they had shot up like antennae trying to pull thoughts from the air. Maybe it could work. All he needed was a couple of sentences that would satisfy her enough to stop the tough questions he didn't want to answer.

"We don't have much to go on right now," Frank said. "There are several reports on missing women, but none of them, except for the one on Stella, I mean, even come close to this victim's description. We're talking based on her size, race, and so forth."

He was thinking, *So far, so good.* He was encouraged.

"We can't get dental records for a few days. As it stands now, a positive ID by someone who knew her would help move this along."

Something in Theo's stomach started to rumble – she couldn't tell which end of her anatomy needed to embrace the commode first. She sat down, hoping the parked position would suppress one urge; then she started the slow breathing technique to control the building nausea.

This can't be true, she thought. It was a mental plea grasping at hope. But as Theo had learned the hard way over too many years, the truth is unavoidable. Truth is its own reality, and wishing it away doesn't make it so.

When Stella didn't show up for the better part of a week, Theo had hoped for a simple explanation. She figured that she'd gone off with a friend to Las Vegas or was camping in Arizona with some of her environmentalist buddies, or any one of a dozen preferred alternatives. She even imagined that maybe Stella had reconciled with her family and gone home to Los Angeles. These were all happy options – just nothing Frank was offering her right now.

"My gut said something wasn't right." Theo was mumbling more to herself than to Frank.

"It just wasn't like her to just take off and not let Abby or me know where she was going."

In Frank's business, a phone call like this was something that cops did all the time. It just never got easier. The dread and humiliation that partners grief when the death is the result of mysterious circumstances was always discernable even over the phone.

"Look . . . Theo," it was a cautious start, "you get what's at stake here. I know you do. I don't want to put you through any more than is absolutely necessary. I wish to God that I didn't have to ask this. But we need someone to take a look. Someone to say 'no, that's not her,' and then we could begin checking other leads. It would really help. It would get us started."

"So you're saying it's *not* her?"

"I'm saying we need someone to *tell* us that."

"And that someone's me?"

"We don't really have any one else to ask."

"Uh-huh. So *this* is *all* you want me for?"

Frank was thinking about baseball – specifically those hard-line drives that can crack skulls. He mentally hit the dirt.

Theo was thinking about recent history – theirs. It was a chapter she didn't ever expect to open again. But here he was forcing the issue. She wasn't sure which was worse – Frank trying to sound like a friend gently guiding her around the horrific details, or Frank the cop getting his bottom line by finagling her cooperation. It wasn't a decision; it was a nightmare. She just wanted to rewind the tape, start over, go back to bed so she could dismiss it all – Stella's missing, the dead woman who might or might not be Stella, and dealing with any of it through Frank.

He was saying, "Listen, I understand if you don't want to, but *Theo*." It was how he whispered her name. It sounded almost like a caress; then, he said the magic word, "*Please*."

She took a deep breath, held it, and then exhaled slowly.

"So the purpose of your call was just to ask me to identify this woman who may or may not be Stella, *right*? That's *all* this is about?"

Frank hesitated. He wanted to say that this was about so much more. To tell her how many times he'd started to call. To number the nights he'd gotten in the car, driven over to her place, and then cruised by without stopping. The uncountable drafts he'd begun on paper that wound up littering his floor. In the end, he just gave up. Now, with the distance of time separating them, with the hurt still so close to the surface, he couldn't let his guard down. He didn't dare. There was just no going back. He took a mental deep breath, cleared his throat.

"Yeah, I guess that's what this is about."

At that precise moment, like two trains on parallel tracks – one headed north, the other south – they each moved on.

"OK," she said. "When?"

Stunned, Frank mumbled a tentative, *"Tomorrow?"*

Tomorrow sounded far enough way, but Theo eyed the digital readout on her clock. It was only a little after 3:00 a.m. She marveled at how her world had lurched on its axis in the space of a few short minutes. But worse, since it was already here, the prospect of tomorrow was even more immediate and threatening.

"It's already tomorrow."

"Yeah, well, I meant later tomorrow." Then he said, "Would it help if Abby came with you?"

Theo said she thought that might be good idea.

Actually, Frank thought it was brilliant – the thought of being alone with her only presented problems he couldn't work out at the moment. When Frank said he'd drive them both, Theo balked. The last thing she wanted was to sit in the passenger seat of Frank's squad car, trying to make ridiculous small talk. The idea was about as welcome as a mammogram. But then, she thought about Stella. *What if it really is Stella?*

A picture of the beautiful smiling Stella flashed in her thoughts and was gone as quickly as it came leaving her with a different sight, the vision of a sheet-wrapped corpse shielding an unspeakable horror.

Theo shuddered. Her insides felt like ice, and she started to sweat. It was a panic attack, and her chest was already beginning to tighten up, choking her, forcing her to gulp shallow gasps of air. Theo did what she'd trained herself to do when this happened, something she'd done since junior high. She forced herself to hold her breath and count to twenty. It was a simple maneuver and allowed her lungs to inflate. Slowly, she could feel her chest opening up, allowing longer, deeper breaths. The clamminess started to subside.

Now she could concentrate on Frank's voice. He was saying, "I really think I should drive you both, if that's OK?"

Theo snagged Frank's offer of a ride like a lifeline – it mentally stabilized her thoughts. She conceded that it was sensible and practical, especially with the prospect of Abby being there.

"You're right. OK."

"How about nine tomorrow, I mean today?" Frank offered.

"Sure."

She started to hang up, but he was still on the line. Once again, the silence was a specter's presence between them. She waited; hoping to God there wasn't more.

CHAPTER 2

"**O**K, I'll see you at nine then," Frank said.

She didn't respond. He said, "Theo?"

"Sure. Nine." She said, snapping her phone shut.

Frank switched off his own cell and threw it on the desk. He stared at it like *it* was the offender. He reached for the mug of lukewarm coffee, winced at the acrid taste but swallowed anyway. Frank dreaded making the call to Theo ever since being summoned to the slough to view the human remains under the makeshift tarp.

He'd known it was Stella the instant he saw the short tousled hair spilling out from under the yellow plastic sheet. Even wet and tangled with the backwater debris, in the cool dry air the exposed locks had begun to reclaim their curl as if trying to summon up the life that had deserted them. Odd that he should recognize them now. It certainly hadn't been the curls that he recalled from their first meeting. The mental image was vivid.

It was a warm San Diego evening. He and Theo were leaving her cottage, heading out to dinner. Stella had just returned from a run and bounced over to greet them. She was flushed with a few beads of perspiration running down her neck and into the cleavage between her breasts. She could have been on the cover of the *Sports Illustrated* swimsuit edition. She looked sexy and just out of reach. He felt his gut twinge and hoped his mouth wasn't gaping open.

Right then and there Frank figured that Stella was trouble. She looked like the kind of girl that could reel you in and you'd never feel the hook – you'd be done for and wouldn't know it until you started to bleed. He could tell she was a pro at it.

Frank found himself absently moving through the motions of the introductory "hellos" and small talk all while he thought his blood pressure must be topping 260.

He'd struggled to focus on her eyes and carry on a simple three-way conversation, but his gaze was drawn down the gentle curve of her waist, firm and golden, where her tight running shorts were slung low on her hips. The lip of a belly button was seductively nestled in that exposed smooth stomach lightly dusted with soft blonde fuzz. He'd managed to keep his senses sharp enough to figure that with enough rope she could tie men in knots. His plan was not to be one of them. That was the first time he'd met Stella.

The second time he saw her, she was dressed in a brown sleeveless V-neck sweater cinched in at the waist with a wide leather belt. The sweater slipped down over her hips, topping a leopard-print silk skirt. The skirt fell in tiers of ruffles just above her knees and fluttered as she walked across the terrace of Bobby Galpino's high-rise balcony overlooking San Diego's waterfront.

He recalled how each *click, clack* of her stiletto-heeled sandals on the Italian tile sounded like gunshot. If she recognized him, it just might have been.

He felt his breath stick in his chest as she moved toward him, flashing a smile that could blind and acting like she'd never seen him before in her life.

Frank gratefully swallowed his big sigh of relief and played it straight too. Later, he figured she either really didn't remember him, or she too had a secret life she kept from Bobby.

Whatever the reason for his reprieve that day, something was dangerously out of whack – Galpino's playmate was also Theo's friend. The thought was as welcome as a poke in the eye. It was an ugly twist of fate, an unfortunate coincidence, and it made his work and his private life line up like a cue shot with Galpino holding the stick.

It was enough to start that tiny alarm in his brain twitching – his cop's warning sensor was going off and that always meant "trouble – watch it!" Not long after that, Stella went missing.

Suddenly his phone vibrated a buzzing dance across his desk, jerking him back to the present.

"Yeah!" He mumbled.

"Frank," the deep male voice said his name softly. "Haven't heard from you for a couple days, we still on?"

Hearing Bobby Galpino's voice while he had been deep in thought about Stella was creepy.

"Bobby." Frank mustered a friendly tone, "Shit! Meant to call, just been busy on the crack house detail. If my shit-for-brains captain would just get off my ass about busting the chops of every stupid son of a bitch that smokes that shit I could concentrate on the important things around here! So enough about me! Hell yes, I'm in. Thursday. Right?"

"That's the plan," Galpino said, "Thursday. You know the place."

Frank wanted to grill Bobby about Stella's disappearance and her death, but now wasn't the time, and he stifled the urge. That part of his job would have to wait. Right now, he had to attend to the business at hand.

"Catch you Thursday then, Frank," Bobby Galpino said and clicked off.

Frank glanced at his watch. It was almost 5:00 a.m. He had a little time to grab a few winks before he picked up Theo. He groaned at the thought of facing her.

Discounting this morning, it seemed like years since they'd last spoken; taking her to the morgue was not the reunion he had planned. He just hoped they could get through the ordeal without lapsing into one of their knock-down-drag-outs. *Maybe that wouldn't be so bad,* he thought, recalling how they often had to "agree" to disagree especially about politics and how making up had been more than worth the effort. *Like that's going to happen!*

Frank stood, yawned and stretched, then headed for the elevator.

CHAPTER 3

Theo cupped both hands around the thick ceramic mug and breathed in the steam rising from her coffee. It worked to clear her stuffy nose a little and ward off the sinus pressure that was building.

Leaning against the window sill, she listened to the metallic creak of the *Las Casitas* plaque swinging on its iron trellis. It was comforting background noise, like the whip snap of the palm tree fronds in the wind.

Ordinarily, early morning was Theo's special time. It was the best for writing. She used the darkness like a blackboard to sketch out her thoughts without distractions. This morning's scene would have been idyllic except for Frank's phone call and what was waiting for her at the morgue. There was no mental escaping what lay ahead. It hung on her like wet germs – disgusting and lethal.

Any normal person would have hoped for a positive outcome. Theo wanted that too; it just wasn't like her to reach for anything but the facts. That's something she learned in her thirty-two years. Expecting good news in the face of certain tragedy was nothing more than a diet of candy versus a healthy balance of protein and carbs – it was a fantasy. It produced the sugar spike that precedes the plunge into a glycemic free fall. In the end, there's always the consequence of the plummeting crash.

Theo didn't play games with her psyche. She didn't set herself up for a pitiful fall. Rather, she faced the bad news squarely, took her blows, and moved on. That had been her motto, and she worked hard at sticking to it. It was, after all, the smart thing to do, and it was what her grandmother taught her.

"Some hurts deserved to be buried" was how her grams had explained it, "and being on the right side of the shovel is better than the alternative!"

Theo shook her head and half smiled at the echo of her grandmother's advice. It was that Midwest common sense approach that had always worked both for her grandmother and for her. It was how she sorted out the facts. It was how she arrived at a solid conclusion. It was how she survived as an investigative reporter, and she was good at it.

But this morning was special in a different, unwelcome way. All rationality teetered on the opposite end of the seesaw. Theo was caught between a plea for Stella's well-being and the gnawing fear that she might be dead. She didn't get to be detached and calloused about it. So like it or not, Theo was suspended in a temporary purgatory of hope – the vacuous space between heaven and hell – and that's where she'd be until she knew for sure.

At the window, she gazed at the cottage across the patio, unit 2 – Stella's place. She remembered how excited Stella had been when she first saw it. How she gushed paragraphs over the lush garden setting. Stella even pointed out that the turquoise doorway was like "a little french kiss of color wrapped in the warm hug of the caramel exterior."

Theo was reminded of something else Stella said that day. The oddness of it stuck and seemed as ominous as the roll of thunder.

"It's my own secret place!" Stella had muttered almost under her breath.

"Who or what were you hiding from, Stella?" Theo wondered aloud, "And what went wrong?"

The wind picked up and rattled the *Las Casitas* plaque again. Theo welcomed the *squeak, squawk* segue and went with it.

She thought how descriptive a name can be. In Spanish, *Las Casitas* meant "the little houses." And the complex was as homey as the vernacular implied. Six bungalows flanked a central courtyard, each with their own view of the bougainvillea-draped pergola. There were benches and a fountain with its soft tumble of water. The reality completed a picture that could have been the focal spread for *Better Homes and Gardens.*

Growing up, Theo thought it was a wonderland, a cozy village – quiet and safe – with its prefabricated family of tenants chosen by Grandmother Julia who selected them as carefully as some might buy diamonds. Even now, it was her protected haven, a niche for private lives tucked away in the exclusive Mission Hills neighborhood.

Just then, a finch swooped past her window and disappeared into a crevice in the vine's twisted canopy.

Right on cue, she thought.

The breeze ruffled the petunias in the hanging baskets on the porch of unit 2 once more. Theo made a mental note to water them later.

Later, she thought, *later, I'll be in the passenger seat of Frank's squad car, heading to the morgue.* She shivered trying to shake off the dismal prospect.

They say that the threat of bad news is almost as devastating as the final dénouement. In a few hours, she would know if that was true. Frank asking her to identify the woman's body and the horrifying possibility that it might be Stella was the sucker punch of dilemmas.

She squeezed and released her shoulders to relieve the building tension, as if that purposeful act could expel Stella from the dreadful equation. As if the agonizing dread associated with Stella wasn't bad enough, she also had to deal with the annoyance of Frank in the picture.

Theo worked especially hard at not stirring up old memories of Frank. Like the muddy sediment in the bottom of a bottle of wine, they were murky, confusing, and only clouded her plan for her future without him.

He was the one who had said good-bye; she had come to accept it. After he walked away, she wanted to curl up in a ball and die. It took months to banish the memories of what they once had and lost. Only a few moments on the phone revealed how close to the surface those feelings remained. It was like staring at a giant ache, an open sore, a rip in her soul.

Until his call, she thought she was way past the healing point. Hearing his voice again was like ripping off the band aid. Feeling the pain again made her just plain pissed.

Damn steam! She thought, as if blaming it for her runny nose and watery eyes would make it so. The last thing she wanted was tears and sniffles. She blew her nose, wiped the moisture from her eyes, and tossed the Kleenex into the wastebasket, dismissing it and Frank.

KC, her gray tabby, sauntered into the kitchen and plopped on his haunches by his food bowl. He waited expectantly. She welcomed the interruption, opened a packet of *Whisker Lickin's*, and dumped them in the cat's bowl. She grabbed the coffeepot and topped off her mug.

A soft halo of reddish golden light began to outline the roof of Stella's unit and stain the clouds forming on the horizon.

"Red skies in the morning, sailors take warning," Theo mumbled, "red skies at night, sailor's delight."

It was something her grams used to say when she predicted a change in the weather. Then, just as quickly, a verse from Shakespeare's *Macbeth* came to mind, "Something evil this way comes."

"Well, there's a cheery thought!" she muttered, shrugging off the sudden chill. Theo picked up the phone and dialed Abby.

CHAPTER 4

Bobby Galpino paced his seventeenth-floor terrace overlooking the waterfront and harbor. He snubbed out a cigarette butt on the terrace balustrade and flicked it over the side. He was expecting his cell phone to ring, and waiting was something he was not good at. Finally, the phone vibrated on his belt.

"Yeah," Bobby barked. "Where the hell you been?"

"Hey, Bobby, listen, man, I'm sorry, got hung up here at the club. I had a shitload of paperwork and – "

Bobby cut him off midsentence.

"Fuck that crap. So where are we on the deal?"

"Man, we're all set. I'm just waiting for him to show up. This thing will button up and be history. You gotta trust me, Bobby, I'm on top of it."

Bobby snorted a half laugh.

"Shit, you Bozo, you never did anything that was 'buttoned up.' I'm warning you, Angel, you blow this, and we'll both be mincemeat. So you stay on it and call me as soon as it's a slam-dunk. Clear?"

"Sure, sure, Bobby, honest, don't worry."

Bobby snapped his phone shut and stared out at the view. The harbor was coming to life with a couple of tugs moving a barge south, probably headed to the Thirty-second Street Naval industrial center.

He considered what could go wrong with his plan and ticked off every precaution he'd taken. Angel Martinez was no Einstein, but he was like family – he and Angel went way back to the old neighborhood. He could be counted on to follow directions, plus, he was scared shitless of Bobby's Las Vegas connection, not to mention Uncle Louie. So was Bobby. Following the rules was how Uncle Louie expected Bobby to play the game. With Uncle Louie, blood was thicker than water – but screwups got dealt with – quickly and permanently. Bobby didn't plan to get sent to the woodshed with Uncle Louie's boys.

Bobby knew his part. It was the last piece in a complicated plan, and he was banking on the "Juggernaut" to button it up. Juggernaut hadn't been Bobby's choice for bagman, but the decision to hire this professional hadn't been his anyway. Now, with success so close, he wanted to relax a little.

Bobby watched a cruise ship glide across the bay toward port. He thought of his yacht, and that brought up memories of Stella. Bobby hadn't seen Stella for a few weeks, partly because he'd been busy and partly because he didn't like to let women think they owned him.

When he had started to feel differently about Stella, like wanting to see her and not just for sex, to spend time with her, maybe even introduce her to some of his family, he fought the urge. He had to be careful with her. Introducing a girl into the family circle had an implied meaning, like a permanent relationship. Bobby wasn't sure he was ready for that, yet. He was, after all, Bobby Galpino, a very powerful man. She was, well, she was lots of things, but nothing Bobby figured he couldn't handle. Stella was fun, and he figured after a little hiatus she'd be anxious to see him.

Maybe we'll take a little cruise up to Catalina, she'd like that, Bobby thought. He pictured lounging on his yacht with Stella sunning herself, maybe with her top off. That started a warm sensation that made him smile.

Bobby flipped his phone open, pressed the speed dial for her number, and waited until her voice mail message chirped on.

"Hi, you've reached *me*, but I'm not available right now. Leave me a message, and I'll call you back! *Ciao for now!*"

When Stella didn't answer, he mumbled an expletive and hung up. Bobby never left messages on answering machines or voice mail. He was careful about that. Anyone in his line of work would be.

CHAPTER 5

The décor was retro-industrial drab just what you'd expect for a morgue. Chrome chairs sported hospital green vinyl seats. You couldn't call them cushions; there was nothing *cushy* about them. They were designed to force you to sit at attention; then dismiss you after your worst fears were confirmed.

Theo felt the substance of dread in the small space suspended in the air like a tangible presence; it was the fear of not knowing, and it shrouded those who had been summoned there to put a name to the dead. Like Scrooge's *Ghost of Christmas Yet to Come*, it silently stretched a boney finger pointing into the future – an ominous signal of the desolate prospect that lay ahead.

Theo and Abby sat without speaking. Abby was stoic. Theo fidgeted.

Abby Archer had been Theo's friend since fourth grade. Their lives were a scrapbook of memories – grade school cliques, high school intrigues laced with teenage hysterics and drama, college exploits and long-night discussions in flannel pajamas, munching popcorn while they solved the world's problems or at least decided what to do about each other's current significant romantic involvement.

They had always been there for one another during the good times and the bad. Theirs was a bond tighter than friendship – they were blood, a family of their own choosing.

Theo stared straight ahead at their reflections in the glass of the floral print whose greens had sun-faded to blue. Abby's close-cropped dark hair, prematurely sprinkled with gray and worn slightly spiked in front, accented her strong-boned features.

Theo had always admired the clear hazel eyes that stared at life's challenges from behind wire-rimmed glasses without flinching. If she were composing a character study for a personal's ad, Theo would sum Abby up like this: energetic and always poised to win, a woman who took life with her feet firmly planted, whether it was taking a roiling wave precision-balanced atop her surfboard, or dishing out her usual stick-in-your-eye advice to customers at Bailey's – Abby Archer was solid and unflappable. Hers was a gutsy zest for life powered by a rocket thrust drive.

Theo sighed, more fidgeting. Too much time on one's hands lends itself to nervous thoughts that twist and meander through craziness. Theo's concentration rambled around in twitchy corridors. She scanned and dissected the morgue's décor. She assessed Abby's admirable attributes and then turned introspective – like picking at a scab that itches.

She stared critically at her own reflection. *God, just look at me, a disheveled and pathetic blob.* She mentally groaned.

Her shoulder-length auburn hair, which had been hastily pulled back into a knot at the nape of her neck, was unraveling from its elastic band. The deep brown eyes, usually one of her better features, sunk into shadow in a face that was pale and haggard.

Theo pressed the sides of her face with both hands and ovaled her mouth to see how much she resembled *Edvard Munch's Scream. OK,* she thought, *that's a stretch.* She smirked at her own pun.

Theo felt like a poster child for anxiety. She couldn't sit still. She alternated between leg twitching, exhaling sharp gusts through lips that sputtered like a small boat engine and blowing her nose into a wad of Kleenex. Finally, Abby squeezed her hand with a small gesture of reassurance. Theo managed a nervous smile.

"I know I'm acting like a two-year-old." Theo simpered apologetically.

"You're good at it," whispered Abby.

Theo rewound her hair then blew her nose once more.

They both just waited.

After what seemed like an interminable stretch, Frank, who had stepped out of the room earlier, reentered with a woman in a lab coat and introduced her as Dr. Weiss, the coroner. Weiss escorted them into a small room with a draped window. She spoke to someone via a wall phone then hung up.

"Are you OK to do this?" She asked kindly.

The pair nodded cautiously in sync.

The curtain was pulled back. An attendant on the other side of the glass partition slowly raised the sheet, exposing the head of the corpse. Theo gasped. The woman's hair had been combed straight back from her bloated pasty white face that looked like a plaster death mask only not as flattering; the ugly purple marks on her neck didn't even register with Theo.

"I . . . I don't know." Theo stammered and glanced at Abby for reassurance. Abby said nothing, but stared at the corpse with a slight glimmer of recognition.

Dr. Weiss cleared her throat and spoke next, "Does your friend have any identifying marks like moles or scars? A tattoo perhaps?"

The image of Stella, tanned and vibrant as she jogged with the raspy sounds of Pink Floyd buzzing from earphone jacks, her back glistening from sweat and the butterfly tattoo perfectly centered above the band of her running shorts, flashed like a snapshot.

"Stella has a tattoo," Theo offered, "a tiny butterfly, in the small of her back."

The doctor picked up the phone and repeated that to the attendant who nodded. She closed the drapes and waited until the red buzzer on the phone sounded. When the drapes were pulled back, the sheet had been rearranged so that it covered everything except a small area of the back.

In the expanse of dead flesh, the butterfly was poised; its red, purple, and yellow colors were vivid, happy, and beautifully alive – as if it could have lifted off and fluttered away.

Theo swallowed, trying to dislodge the knot in her throat then nodded in affirmation. The drapes closed again.

"Thank you, Ms. Hunter," Dr. Weiss said. "That will help the police with their investigation."

"Investigation?" Theo's voice was a croaky whisper.

Frank and Weiss exchanged glances.

"Theo," Frank said, measuring his tone to calibrate the impact, "the coroner will need to determine the cause of death. It's a simple formality."

"Yes, of course it is," Theo said, still staring at the drawn curtain, unable to dispel the thought of the body on the other side of the glass.

Then, almost as an afterthought, "I don't think *my* ID is all you should go on for a positive. What about fingerprints? Those would be more reliable?" Theo pleaded, hoping that fingerprint forensics would prove her wrong. A butterfly tattoo was popular among many young women, and this could simply be a horrible coincidence. The rush of hope was obvious.

Weiss hesitated before answering, but she was candid.

"Fingerprints, of course, would help. Unfortunately, in this case, there has been a great deal of damage to the hands. Fingerprints" – she paused as if to lessen the impact of the obvious, but naturally, it had the opposite effect – "are unavailable. After so many days subjected to the water, currents, shoreline rocks, and other forces, it is not unusual for a body to be damaged in such a way that identifying marks, such as fingerprints, can't be obtained. When that happens, we rely on verification by family or friends. We will, of course, contact the deceased's relatives and obtain dental records for confirmation. Your witness at this point is helpful in starting that process."

Theo nodded absently and started for the door.

"I'm really sorry," Frank said looking at the two women. "There was the chance that we were mistaken."

CHAPTER 6

From the top level of the Horton Plaza Shopping Center parking structure, Jarvis Barkley leaned against the grill of his sleek Jaguar. Through binoculars, he scanned the warehouse district from Sixteenth Street south to Island and made a mental note to add those few blocks to his planned redevelopment project.

Barkley considered himself to be every inch the land baron's Renaissance man. If anything, his accomplishments supported his high opinion of himself.

He was one of the most prolific developers in San Diego County. He owned Barkley Square Hotel and Convention Center just east of La Jolla and Interstate 5 in the golden triangle area, and he'd recently built the Equinox, a high-rise condominium compound in the upscale historical Gaslamp area of downtown, where he was the sole occupant of the $5 million dollar penthouse. He dressed and looked the part – Armani suits, a stable of expensive cars – and a lesser known fact – he had a penchant for exotic-looking young men.

Barkley retrieved the small metal object from his pocket, raised it to his lips, and kissed both sides of the two-headed gold coin. Barkley would never consider initiating any business deal without performing this good-luck ritual. It was his providential talisman and, thus far, it had only brought him success.

Barkley was compulsive about respecting the good-versus-evil conundrum. He believed it too was a two-headed coin of sorts. He made sure that he kept the perfect balance between the two.

On one side, he bought politicians. This he did by supporting their campaigns, gifting them with expensive trinkets and other valuables and treating them to guest seats in his pricey boxes at Qualcomm Stadium and PETCO Park. He bankrolled college scholarships for their kids. And as further proof of the extent of his influence, he secured their appointments to powerful commissions and committees.

On the opposite side of the coin, Barkley supported the local homeless mission. For this charitable generosity, he was frequently pictured in the local press and dubbed San Diego's "Philanthropic Godfather." Barkley readily accepted the title and saw it as proof that his cosmic balancing act was a perfect adaptation of Newton's law of reciprocal actions. Specifically, that all forces occur in pairs and that these two forces are equal in magnitude and opposite in direction.

Barkley reasoned that his application of the laws of physics was brilliant and absolute proof of his superiority. He suffered from the same flaw common in antisocial pathological reasoning and was not troubled by any nagging doubts of conscience.

His most recent venture would certainly support that. Barkley had manipulated the last election go-round to ensure the success of his most recent project. He supported the city council incumbents and made enormous donations to their campaign chests from his several dummy corporations. To insure their success at the polls, he launched a smear campaign against their opponents. Barkley had an army of public relations gurus at his disposal and he made good use of them. A little indiscretion can be made into a colossal brouhaha with the right spin. It worked, of course; salacious hit pieces usually do. Barkley's incumbents won by a huge margin.

As if to further support Barkley's claim to cosmic supremacy, a recent ruling by the United States Supreme Court upholding the eminent domain statutes added one more plus to Barkley's side of the balance sheet. Luck was on his side again. He didn't know who had bankrolled the high court's decision – he just figured someone had – but whatever it was that motivated that verdict, it simplified Barkley's redevelopment strategy and set him up for gold.

With a little prompting, he convinced his bought politicians to declare fifteen blocks of prime real estate in downtown San Diego as blighted areas. Then, Barkley purchased them at well below market value.

It's just damn good Providence! Barkley reasoned.

Barkley pressed the speed dial on his cell phone. After two rings he connected.

"Juggernaut!" The male voice answered.

Barkley thought it sounded a little slurred. "I *do* love the sound of that! Almost takes my breath away." He cooed into the receiver.

"Not your type, Barkley," was the clipped response.

"Ah." Barkley feigned an exaggerated sigh, "such a pity. Oh well then, what *do* you have for me?"

"Feldspar's in."

"Excellent!" Barkley grinned.

"When do I pick up the package?" asked Juggernaut.

"I'll call you and set up a time in a day or two. Did you ever take care of that little matter of our unhappy *entertainer?*"

"She's no longer a problem," was Juggernaut's curt reply.

"Ah," said Barkley, "taken her final bow shall we say, excellent again."

Juggernaut had no patience for Barkley's snide remarks. "We'll connect later." With that, Juggernaut hung up.

Barkley thrust his face into the salty breeze and inhaled. *That's the sweet smell of success, and I'm one lucky son of a bitch.* He held his two-headed talisman to his lips and let his kiss linger on the cold metal before slipping it back into his pocket.

Now he was poised and ready for the final countdown.

CHAPTER 7

Juggernaut contemplated his next step. He hadn't planned things to turn out as they had, but then, his whole life had been a sequence of events that he didn't orchestrate. He followed the road laid out before him, and it all just fell into place like connecting the dots. Some might call it dumb luck. He called it karma.

With his first sip of scotch, his thoughts moved from Stella backward to his youth.

His name had not always been Juggernaut. He'd heard it somewhere as a kid and liked how it evoked the image of pure energy. He pictured Juggernaut having an identity – a superhero's body like a bright yellow-orange lightning bolt, sharp and jagged as a knife, threatening and invincible. "Juggernaut" became his alter ego, his all-powerful "avatar."

Until the time he adopted his special persona, life had been a sequence of one bad scene after another. It was tough times for a kid like him – no father and a mother with a sixth-grade education. Her job opportunities were sparse; she was lucky to work the janitorial night shift at an insurance company on Wilshire Boulevard in Los Angeles.

Her days were spent sleeping, usually after downing a bottle of Night Train, a cheap wine that could peel varnish off finished wood. He was on his own and subject to everything and everyone in the raw East Los Angeles neighborhood.

He was the gang gopher to the older kids; he stole candy and cigarettes from the local convenience stores for the boss-leaders. To gain higher rank, he'd have to work his way up from petty theft to the prize jobs – the dangerous ones – but at thirteen, that promotional break was a long way off.

So he just limped along – the punching bag for the higher-ups, the bullied kid, the wimp.

One day, he saw the Yin-Yang symbol on a billboard ad for cheap liquor. Like a sign from heaven, it grabbed his attention. When he saw it again on an astrology magazine in a rack at the local 7-Eleven, he snatched it. Later, he read a couple of the horoscopes and liked the concept that life's vagaries could be explained by the juxtaposition of the stars and planets. He discovered that his August 1 birth date made him a Leo. Symbolized by the lion, he took that to mean that he was a leader, not a follower. His battered self-image began to perk up.

He looked up the Yin-Yang symbol and found that it represented the ancient Chinese understanding of how things worked. The black yin and white yang symbols within a circle were the interaction of two energies – black represented the weak, passive side of life, while white stood for the energetic strong side. One *accepted* everything around it, the other *made* things happen.

By the time he finished the article, he had a sort of Yin-Yang rebirth. Juggernaut decided that from that point on he would be the force that made things happen. He deduced that, like the quintessence of Yin-Yang, his power could not exist without the opposite energy.

Thus, he reasoned, he must always have someone close to him to embody the passive *acted upon* segment of the circle. He would always need someone to domineer. He began to scheme how he might change the dynamic of his present circle of existence to match his new philosophy. He was currently the *yin*; he had to become the *yang*. As luck would have it, he didn't discover the way out – it found him.

After a series of successful car thefts, he moved up in the gang-rank echelon advancing to robbery. A foiled holdup attempt at a convenience store got him arrested at fifteen and sent to Central Juvenile Hall, the oldest juvenile detention facility in Los Angeles infamous for its overcrowding and crumbling conditions.

Observation is a key to acquiring the advantage – this was something Juggernaut discovered rapidly. While he awaited arraignment in juvenile court, he learned that kids who had substance abuse problems were often sent to treatment camps or half-way houses, a far better sentence than languishing in any of the regular detention facilities in the county. He formed a plan.

He watched the behaviors of the kids who were alcoholics and mimicked them. He was successful enough to convince his state-appointed attorney to plead a case of alcohol addiction. This was to be the first in a long line of successes in what would become his "acting" career. He was good at it. So good that by the time his detention hearing was held, Juggernaut had convinced everyone that he was a desperate kid in need of rehab, deserving of a second chance away from the influences of the old associations, particularly his alcoholic mother and his gang connections.

Everyone, including the judge, bought it. He was sent to a juvenile camp located in Malibu, a coastal city in Northwest Los Angeles County.

Juggernaut had been right, the camp proved to be a much better environment. It was the perfect chance for a bight kid, and who knows, if he had taken advantage of its opportunities, he might have turned out differently.

Some might argue that he was a bad seed and that no amount of rehabilitation could take out of the flesh what was born into the bone.

Regardless of whether his character was inborn or formed by the mean circumstances of his childhood, the mold was cast; his personality was bent into a pathological inability to empathize with others. This dangerous inclination was hidden behind a handsome and charming exterior, which, much like the young man in Oscar Wilde's *The Picture of Dorian Gray*, his innocent exterior masked the malevolent evil that waited undetected behind an engaging temperament.

In time, he developed into the perfect psychopath.

*   *   *

The phone's staccato bleep cut into his thoughts.

"Juggernaut!"

"I *do* love the sound of that."

It was Jarvis Barkley. Just the sound of his voice grated like fingernails screeching on a chalkboard. If it hadn't been for the money, he would have off'd him just for pleasure.

You sleazy faggot, he thought.

It helped Juggernaut to picture Barkley tied up and worked over with a very sharp knife – it gave him a momentary relief from the anger that was building. Fortunate for Barkley, the transposition worked like a salve on Juggernaut's growing rage. It would be enough to get Juggernaut through the next few days when his work would be completed and his payoff safely in his account in the Cayman Islands.

Then, he thought, *it will be just you and me and this boat. How'd you like a little fishing trip down Mexico way, Jarv baby . . . just the two of us!*

Juggernaut responded to Barkley's questions with robotic efficiency while indulging his mental picture of Barkley staked out naked on a bed. Juggernaut actually stifled a giggle as he imagined Barkley, drunk with silly anticipation, while Juggernaut, stripped naked, straddled him.

Oh, baby, Juggernaut salivated, *and what a look of surprise, Mr. Jarvis Barkley bitch, when I whip out my very big knife!*

Juggernaut tolerated the conversation long enough to confirm the pick up and delivery. But when Jarvis broached the subject of Stella, his mental image went deadly. He dismissed the man and hung up – he had to; the jagged circle on his peripheral vision was starting to grow. It was the thing that preceded his uncontrollable rage, and if he didn't stifle it now, it would consume him. He knew its power – it was his *Juggernaut Avatar* – the all-powerful self – his alter identity – that would avenge Stella and bring down Barkley, and it would be instantaneous, if he didn't stop it.

Juggernaut managed to mentally wrench back control and chided himself. *That would be far too stupid – not now – not before the final payoff.*

He sagged down in the chair, his breathing began to relax. He was beginning to feel in control again and pleased that he'd saved himself a million-dollar bankroll. *That's nothing to toss aside – not for the sake of vengeance or pleasure.* Then he smiled assured that he could still get everything he wanted. *That will come in good time my powerful friend, in very soon and very good time.*

Juggernaut grabbed the Johnnie Walker, topped off his glass, and downed it completely. It felt good and medicinal; it started to loosen up the tightly coiled energy that was ready to blow. He relaxed more knowing that he had controlled what was poised, ready to go when he said it was time. That and the Johnnie Walker was working. He let his thoughts go back. The past was a safer place to be right now. It was where he could range free and safely decompress.

The pounding in Juggernaut's head subsided and his breathing slowed. He savored the quiet, the tender rocking of the boat, the lapping of each gentle wave's caress on its hull. Now, he thought, *now I can turn back to where I was headed before that bastard's call.*

CHAPTER 8

J uggernaut liked reliving his past triumphs – how he learned to use the system to his own advantage. He saw himself as Oscar-worthy in his convincing performance as a youth seeking redemption.

He attended Sunday worship services, learning from each minister the art of connecting with an audience. You might say this was Juggernaut's second epiphany. From it, he developed an uncanny ability to take advantage of the weaknesses of those around him – his peers, his keepers, and his counselors – he used them to his own advantage. Gradually, he was transformed from the street-savvy punk into a calculating manipulator.

A testimony to his accomplished transformation was his camp counselor Elizabeth Trotter. She would be his greatest victory.

Trotter was thirty-something, lonely, and looking for a cause. She fancied herself a Florence Nightingale – a savior – someone who could redeem a smart young subject from the inevitable fate that results from a life of drugs, alcohol, and larceny. Juggernaut seemed vulnerable, pliant, and ready for rescue; naturally, Elizabeth took him on.

"He's a bright, good-looking kid. He has potential. He can change," Elizabeth Trotter reasoned. "I can make a difference in his life!"

Thus, she worked at molding the boy and altering his doomed future. He was her poster child for beating the odds of the mean streets.

Juggernaut saw her as foolish, and that made her his perfect Yang ticket.

Elizabeth worked with him a year. She became confident she had won him over. She liked him. When he revealed his secret Juggernaut name, she thought it was a nickname and shortened it to *Juggie*, thinking it was friendlier and cute.

Outwardly he played cute; inwardly, he hated her and vowed to get even. Juggernaut bided his time, watched, and waited. He gained her trust. Just after his seventeenth birthday, he got his chance.

When Elizabeth Trotter wasn't saving the world, her other passion was studying the classical painters and sculptors of the eighteenth century. She couldn't wait to expose Juggernaut to the phenomenal collection housed at the J. Paul Getty Villa Museum in Malibu. Juggernaut's exemplary behavior and good grades earned him a standing pass for field trips with Trotter.

The Villa's marbled halls became a regular destination for the pair. She allowed herself to revel in the art and antiquities; he luxuriated in the indulgent opulence of unimagined wealth.

While Juggernaut was awed by the incomparable affluence of the oil billionaire's estate turned museum, his passion was studying Elizabeth Trotter. And because she was a devoted romantic more than a dedicated scholar, her obsession became his opportunity.

It was the third visit to the museum that resulted in a life-changing event for both Ms. Trotter and her student.

It was an unusually slow day with just a handful of visitors. The pair studied the Nollekens's *Venus*. The eight-century work depicted the goddess nude to emphasize her beauty and sexual allure. The point wasn't lost on either the teacher or student. It was one of those mesmeric moments when Juggernaut focused on form. The odd light in his eyes as he followed each line of the sculpture, fixating on the cold-hard breasts and thighs, caught Elizabeth slightly off guard. She was uncomfortable and moved on.

At Antonio Canova's sculpture of *Apollo*, Elizabeth became oddly short winded. Perhaps it was the exquisite muscular strength of this marble god enthralled with his own nude perfection and crowning himself with a laurel wreath that ratcheted her blood pressure to over 200. The sense of flushed excitement rapidly upshifting to arousal made her weak. She desperately needed air.

At that perfect moment, Juggernaut was beside her. His eyes bored into her. When he pressed closer, her every nerve tingled from their bodies' heat. She felt suffocated, unsteady on her feet. Juggernaut took control. He guided her out into the cool breeze of the columned piazza. He acted kind and concerned. She bought it. The next sequence of events proceeded as if scripted.

The pair quickly left the museum and headed for Elizabeth's cozy bungalow, an unattached studio-sized guest house that she rented in Coral Canyon. Its garden setting afforded quiet and privacy, the perfect setting for what would become a frequent and private interactive life-science class for teacher and student.

Juggernaut reveled in the turn of fate that resulted in the best luck he could have imagined. He soon learned every possible way to excite and satisfy her.

She eagerly surrendered. His appetite was ravenous, insatiable, and dominant. She bought it all – the erotic historical romance, the dangerous illicit affair.

Juggernaut liked the sex – he reveled in the perfect triumph of his personal Yin-Yang. Things could not have been better for either of them and might have continued for years and years if it had not been for one little mistake – Elizabeth trusted him.

She might have fantasized about him turning eighteen and them getting married. She might have expected to continue her happy, fulfilled life into her eighties with a young doting Juggie by her side, caring for her. She might have believed that he loved her, that he was even capable of love. Whatever her fanciful imaginings, she trusted him beyond any grayscale of doubt. Before long, he had complete access to her home and her bank account.

The idyllic odyssey lasted a year. Juggernaut's eighteenth birthday approached. The courts would consider him emancipated and eligible for dismissal from the Malibu camp if he were judged rehabilitated. Everyone was convinced he was ready to enter society. When he was released, he moved into Elizabeth's little bungalow. She was ecstatic. Then, she did something that seemed like the right next step. It was to be a devastating wrong turn. It sealed the foolish woman's fate forever.

After an early morning sexual romp, she whispered, "I want to make you a permanent part of my life."

Juggernaut was bored and only half listened until he heard, "I have a trust fund for your college education and," she nibbled on his ear, "I've made you my sole heir, darling!"

He couldn't believe the rush. Now *he* was ecstatic. He returned kisses and made love to her until, exhausted, she slept.

Juggernaut lay beside his benefactress and considered what this new bequest meant. He had everything he wanted. His future was secure, but there was one minor obstacle. To gain complete freedom, he needed one thing less. Elizabeth was an unnecessary appendage. There was no inward debate; Elizabeth Trotter had to go.

Elizabeth always showered before bed. When she stepped out of the shower that night, Juggernaut was waiting with two glasses of champagne. He offered her the one laced with several dissolved Vicodins. She passed out before finishing the second dose. He slipped her bikini on her and drove the short distance to the beach. It was 2:00 a.m. and deserted.

He carried her out beyond the pounding surf to where the swells buoyed her body making it easy to guide. When he let her go, Juggernaut was surprised at how easily she slipped beneath the water and disappeared. He paddled around for a few minutes until he was sure Elizabeth didn't resurface.

*   *   *

Juggernaut drained his glass and poured another. He savored the liquid as it slid down his throat with a slight burn. He raised his glass in a toast to Elizabeth whom he thought of as his mentor and first total conquest.

Since Elizabeth, he'd managed to have the upper hand with all of them. They always trusted him. And he used them any way he wanted. It worked with Elizabeth and later with Stella.

He was past getting drunk.

Thoughts of Stella started a warm, tingly arousal. He mentally switched gears.

It was damn bad luck that she fell for that Delaney asshole, he thought. *She was just plain stupid.*

Killing Stella was not part of the original plan, but as he saw it, she became a liability when she forgot who she was. As with Elizabeth, his options for Stella were clear. He had no choice, no chance for a debate.

Again, he mused about not letting a cool million slide through his fingers.

You shouldn't have double-crossed me, baby, it was your fatal flaw.

Juggernaut justified the change in plans as being dictated solely by the money factor.

If the money hadn't been at stake, I could have just punished you – it wouldn't have been the first time.

But, he reasoned, *Barkley's plan was too delicate to toy with.*

I really wish it could have been different, baby, he mumbled raising his glass in a final toast to Stella, *looks like your Yin simply ran out.*

CHAPTER 9

It wasn't all that far from the morgue back to Theo's, but so immersed in their own thoughts were Frank and his passengers that it could have been years or seconds – no one seemed to notice. He pulled up in front and switched off the ignition.

Theo stared out the passenger-side window, not focusing on anything in particular; her thoughts lost somewhere in a gray fog.

"Do you know if Stella had any family in town?" Frank asked quietly.

Abby spoke. "As far as I know, her family lived in L.A."

Theo mumbled that she had a phone number on Stella's rent registration card.

"If I could get that from you, we'll contact her parents," Frank said. "Did you ever meet them?"

"No," she said.

"Theo," said Abby. "Listen, I hate to ask this, but I've got to run some errands before I go to work this afternoon. My car's still in the shop. Any chance you could let me use yours?"

Theo nodded, found her keys on the first try which she thought was a minor miracle, and handed them to her.

Abby placed her hand on Theo's shoulder and gave her a reassuring squeeze, "Hey, will you be OK? If you'd like I'll see if I can get someone to cover for me at the club."

"No, don't. There's no need."

Abby gave Frank a raised eyebrow command to stay with her. He nodded.

"OK, if I stay for a while, Theo?" Frank asked.

She looked up at him just as the tears started down her cheeks. She nodded and turned away, fishing around for a Kleenex which wasn't as easy to find as her car keys.

*   *   *

They drank their coffee in silence. Frank made a couple of phone calls to headquarters. She didn't listen to his side of the conversation nor was she focused on anything in particular. Her thoughts seemed dazed and empty with nowhere to go.

A framed photo of Abby, Theo, and Stella taken last year at Sea World caught her eye. She picked it up and handed it to Frank who just ended a call.

"Stella had never been there," Theo said. "We convinced her that seeing *Shamu* was what she had to do – a sort of real San Diego initiation. It was a joke, but she bought it. Stella was like that – gullible. She trusted us."

"We all sat in the front row opposite that ten-million-gallon water tank. As that big fish made his last swing around preparing to leap, Abby and I separated from her like Moses had just parted us. I don't know if she suspected anything, but she never let on. That wave came splashing down on the whole front row and drowned her. She looked like a wet dog. We were all laughing so hard. It was silly, really, just stupid and silly. But it was a great day." She sniffled.

"That's when I snapped the shot. She was laughing and pointing her finger at us, '*You'll get yours one day!*' That's what she said. We never did, though. We never did."

Theo was quiet for moment. She smiled sadly.

"It's hard to believe she won't get even."

Frank watched her top off their coffee. Although he hadn't seen her in months, she looked like he remembered. Even without makeup, Frank thought she was beautiful. Her thick auburn hair had slipped out of its restraint, caressing and framing the line of her neck. He wanted to reach out and gently move it aside. He imagined how she might respond to that, returning his caress with a gentle nuzzle, raising her face toward him, parting her lips, anticipating his kiss.

Given their current status though, he figured if he made a move toward her, she'd just jerk away and freeze him with that icy stare – the one that felt like a hard slap. He shrugged off both images and cleared his throat.

Out of the corner of her eye, Theo watched him too. His jaw twitched slightly as he silently ground his teeth. It was a habit she recognized as something he did just before he said something unpleasant. She settled in the chair opposite the couch where Frank was. He stood up and moved to the kitchen counter. He pulled out his pad and pen.

"Theo," he started, "I'm really sorry. I wish to God that it could be different. But I need to ask you some questions."

She nodded.

He asked about Stella's friends, her associates, and her work. Theo told him what she knew.

"Abby and I were the girlfriends that she hung out with. We shopped, ate out, and went to movies, nothing unique, just girl stuff. Stella worked for an environmental contractor. Other than that, there wasn't too much else. I knew that Stella had some family in L.A. and that her mom died a few years back. But that was it."

"What was her relationship with her dad?"

"Don't really know about her dad. She didn't talk much about him.

"You said 'girlfriends.' Were there boyfriends?"

Theo hesitated. It was enough for Frank to glance up from his notes. He caught the flicker in her eye just before she looked away.

"*Theo*?" Frank asked, trying to push gently.

"This could be critical information. It's going to be hard to backtrack her movements before she died. I'm going to need anything you've got to help me do that." He added softly.

Frank knew Theo would think it was her duty to protect information that she might consider privileged. It was the reporter in her. Somehow he needed to get her to talk.

"No. She didn't have a boyfriend," Theo said.

He was scribbling something on his pad. He didn't look up.

"I think you're lying."

"Yeah? Well, I think you're an asshole!" She shot back. "So clearly what either one of thinks doesn't matter much!"

"Theo, don't mess with this. If you know something and don't tell me its withholding evidence. I could haul you down to headquarters in a hard-ass minute. I don't want to, but I could. This is no time to make your own judgment about what's right or wrong. What you owe Stella right now is helping me find out what happened to her. What we're about here is serious business, not some juvenile game of keeping buddy secrets. Something you think may not be significant could be the key to helping me track her last contacts. She's silent on the matter, but you can speak for her. You're the only one who can." Frank paused, then he added, "Don't let her down."

Theo couldn't believe it. He was trying to pin guilt on her and using her devotion to Stella to make it stick. All the anger that had welled up over these past few months backed up like indigestion. She wanted to scream that he was no expert on friendship. She wanted to yell at him that a real friend wouldn't have deserted her when her life fell apart.

"You make me sick!" was all she could manage to say. "You're hardly the one to take pot shots at someone else. As I recall, you walked away from me when I needed you most. So don't give me that sanctimonious bullshit about loyalty. That word curdles on you!"

"Look, Theo, don't make this about you and me – it's not. It's about a dead girl on the slab in the morgue. I need to know what you know. We'll never put her to rest if we can't figure out what happened. I need your help and so does she."

"She's dead!" Now she was screaming. "Leave her in peace!"

Frank waited for the tears that he knew would follow her outburst – it didn't take long. She grabbed a kitchen towel and wept into it, big painful shudders of grief. It was all he could do – not to seize her and hold on tightly to try to absorb some of the pain, to protect her from the stifling sorrow that gripped her at this moment. Right now, watching her anguished sobbing, more than any other time in his life, it hurt just to know how much he loved her.

He stood by helplessly and waited. After a few moments she stopped. He grabbed a bottle of water from the fridge and handed it to her. She drank a little.

Theo stood facing the window, her reflection a pale ghost of an apparition. She was still for a long time.

"Their affair ended months ago. I don't think it could have anything to do with her death."

"Why not?" Frank tried not to sound incredulous.

She didn't answer.

"Theo? Was he married? Even if there wasn't a wife in the picture if Stella really loved him and they broke up, suicide could be a factor."

"I don't think she'd commit suicide," Theo said matter-of-factly. "It wasn't like her."

"I don't think you know as much about her as you think you do," Frank said watching Theo closely.

"Why would say that?" She was more astonished than insulted.

"Because I think none of us know everything there is to know about someone else or the reasons why they do the things they do. I don't think we can."

"Maybe so," she said under her breath. Then she said, "I promised Stella I'd keep her confidence about him. It's not something that's easy for me to break."

"I know," Frank said quietly, "but the status quo has changed."

Theo thought for a moment.

"He was married."

Frank arched an eyebrow.

"And he was a city councilman."

The hair on his neck bristled. "Go on."

"But he couldn't have had anything to do with," she paused, "her death."

"Maybe. Maybe not. What happened? They break up?" Frank tried to sound calm, but his hand shook a little.

"He told her he was afraid his wife would find out."

"Yeah, they usually do," Frank said. "So who is he?"

"He isn't an *is*," Theo looked Frank squarely in the eye, "Not anymore. He's dead."

CHAPTER 10

"**A**re you talking about *Ted Delaney*?

Theo nodded. "Stella and Delaney were involved. They had to be careful though. He was married, and he was pretty high profile on the city council. Then he broke it off just a couple of days before he died in that accident. I read about the accident in the paper the next morning. I'm the one who told her."

"She was home that morning?"

"Yeah," Theo said, "I woke her. She'd been drinking pretty heavy the night before at Bailey's. She was still trying to get over their breakup. When I told her what happened to Ted, I thought she'd go crazy. I finally got her to take some of that Vicodin I had from my pinched nerve episode. That calmed her down a little, that and the water glass full of scotch she downed. Then, she just cried and cried. Finally, she passed out."

"Theo, try to remember anything she might have said that day?"

"She was so devastated she couldn't talk much."

"Did she say anything about her job?"

"Funny," Theo said, "the most she ever said about her job she said that morning."

"What was that?"

"She said that she should have quit when he asked her to."

"When *who* asked her to?"

"Delaney, I guess."

"Anything else?"

"Just that."

Frank scribbled on his pad. "So did she?"

"No. She stayed on. I told her that she needed to hang in there until she had something else lined up. It's easier to get a job when you already have one. At least that's been my recent experience."

"You would certainly know about that," Frank mumbled under his breath but loud enough so he knew she heard it. Theo ignored it.

"Who else knew about her affair with Delaney?"

"I don't know. I don't think she told anyone else."

"Did she ever mention the name Bobby Galpino?"

"No."

"Did she ever bring Delaney back here?"

"I never saw him. They went out of town to Las Vegas and used different names. I think they were pretty careful." Theo paused, "Who's Bobby Galpino?"

Frank snapped his notepad shut. The interview was over.

"Doesn't matter. Listen, are you sure no one else knew about her and Delaney?"

"Well, I don't think so. Just me, I guess," Theo said thoughtfully.

"You tell anyone? Abby maybe?" Frank eyed her carefully.

Theo was immediately defensive. "Stella confided in me. She trusted me. She knew I wouldn't tell anyone."

"*Right*. So did you?"

She wasn't sure if what she felt was anger or humiliation. He doubted her word. But worse than that insult, he was accusing her of disloyalty to a friend.

"Is that what you think?" She snapped.

He didn't look at her; he just moved for the door.

"I thought you didn't want to make this personal," Theo said.

Frank had his hand on the doorknob but didn't move. His face was dark and unreadable.

"I'm just saying." He let that hang there.

Theo shot him a black look.

He continued, "You'd be surprised how far a tiny shred of gossip can travel. You might have told Abby. She might have told someone she trusts. Those things have a way of getting around, and pretty soon, a whole lot of people know something that only two people knew to begin with. That's all I'm saying."

Theo stood and walked toward him. She felt the sting of angry tears which pissed her off even further; the last thing she wanted was to look vulnerable.

"You don't know me, Frank, obviously, you never did. Why don't we just keep it that way. You should leave now!"

He didn't budge.

"We're not playing games here, Theo. I need to know everything you knew about Stella. Right now, all I have is a dead body and your word that there was an illicit affair with a married politician who also happens to be dead. If you don't see the connection, then you're either not very bright or you're hiding something. So which is it?"

"I told you I don't know anything else!"

"If you think you got hurt before, believe me that was just a scratch compared to ball breakers involved here. This time, it could be *you* on that slab. This is not a game where the big prize is a Pulitzer for a great exposé. This time, it's not about schools or mismanagement of public funds where a few dirty politicians get their hands slapped. This is where the payback is seriously fatal!"

He had the screen door open and was halfway though.

"Theo, if you're hiding something from me so you can play amateur sleuth, you're making a big mistake. You of all people should know how dangerous that is. This is ten times worse than writing tell-all exposes about school board members. That was small potatoes compared to this. Trust me, this one's way out of your league!"

"You don't get to tell me what I can and can't do, but I get to tell you to get the hell out, Frank, and I mean now!"

He let her anger hang in the air between them and waited.

Theo reached for the door handle about to yank it open when Frank grabbed her wrist. His grip was solid as stone and held her midair like she was frozen in place.

"Well, you're right about that," he said quietly.

"So here's what I do get to say. Your friend is dead. You're thinking it's an accident, maybe suicide, and you could be right. Either way, I'm going to find out what happened. *Don't* get in my way."

The screen door slamming couldn't have been as loud as a gunshot, but it sounded just as deadly. With a few choice words, Frank had managed to dredge up all the old pain she had worked so hard to put to rest these past few months.

Theo slumped down on the couch and buried her face in her hands. She coughed up angry painful sobs for Stella and for herself. In those few short minutes, all the work she'd done to erect a dam around her feelings was destroyed and the awful past came flooding in.

CHAPTER 11

The memory of that night was like a bad rerun.

Theo was in the dimly lit bar at the Boat House on Harbor Island, on her second dirty martini, when Frank arrived. He slid into the chair opposite. She quickly used the cocktail napkin to blot her tears.

Frank ordered a scotch. He said nothing. After a couple of gulps, he ordered another. He stared past her at the marina concentrating on the yachts moored there. Theo broke the silence.

"Thanks for coming." She cracked a half smile. "I guess this is my going-away party for two."

"Did you think anyone else would show up?" Frank asked sarcastically. "You're high on the *persona non grata* list, don't you think." It wasn't a question.

She stared at him like he'd just slapped her.

"Frank, you know what happened. I was just trying to find answers to – "

He interrupted. "To what? Life's perplexing problems? Why good people do bad things?" His look registered disgust.

"I was the reporter on the beat when the school shooting happened. All I did was report the facts. The kid got a gun from his father's locked cabinet and shot thirteen people. He killed two kids. He was fourteen years old and had no clue why he did it. I wasn't the only one who wanted to know how it could have gotten to that point!"

She stared out the window, her eyes burning; then the tears started again. Lights on the yachts twinkled in the pale dusk. It was a stage set for romance, whispered secrets between lovers, the hope of love, and the promise of a future. Only this was the wrong script. She felt like she'd just been handed the tragic monologue.

Theo leaned across the table and grabbed his hand, forcing him to make eye contact.

"The truth is that we have no idea who and what we are." Theo began.

"We come together for a few brief hours and act like we're all in sync and then we go off to our homes and whatever heaven or hell that awaits us. Kids do the same. Only they don't always get to know how to make sense out of the shit that terrifies and angers them. That was our job. We had to find out how to reach them. When we set up that counseling website, we got fifty thousand hits the first few weeks. Those teachers and counselors who volunteered their time made a big difference for so many kids. Kids that you'd call normal were just plain scared. They needed someone to talk to. We helped them, and the ones with deeper problems got professional help."

Frank nodded impatiently, then interrupted, "Do you think I don't know how important that was. I was stunned by how everyone pulled together during that hell on earth. You did a great job. I was proud of you."

Theo blew her nose and muttered a slightly slurred "thanks."

Frank took another swallow of his drink and signaled to the bartender. He never had more than two scotches, and now he was having a third. "But I'm not talking about the shooting." His eyes were locked on hers.

"What made you launch some Joan of Arc charge against the establishment? What were you thinking?"

Theo bristled. "I wasn't attacking the *establishment*. I was just doing my job. The political infighting on the school board collided with what we were trying to do to help kids. I exposed it as a hellacious waste of taxpayer money so I could get somebody to listen. When that voting majority on the school board changed, a whole regiment of administrators got canned. It cost multiple six-figure payouts and shoved the whole school program back into the dark ages. Someone had to call it what it was."

She reached for his hand, but it was cold and unresponsive.

"Frank, if I hadn't jumped on that train the next stop would have been banning the word *evolution* from the curriculum! That's how far-out in left field they were heading!"

He pulled his hand away, reached for his glass, and downed it.

"Now it's about *evolution*? Christ, Theo! You don't have the right to tell people what they can or can't preach. You're only responsible for what *you* believe."

"That's where you and I differ, Frank. When it comes to rewriting history, I think I have that right. No! I have that duty!"

"You're not Mahatma Gandhi. You can't change the world."

"Well, I doubt if Dick Bateman would pair me with that great crusader. But thanks!"

"*Bateman?* I'm glad you brought that up." Frank stared at her now, his eyes watery from the scotch and emotion.

"Bateman and his cronies had a field day with you. Hell, it was like a gangbang!" He brought his fist down on the table, and she jumped.

"Do you know how goddamned awful it was to hear you smeared every day on the radio. They labeled you a *dyke and a whore* for *Christ sake!* Oh, you were great material. Hell, Bateman's monologues alone were more popular than Jay Leno's!"

"Glad I could help with his ratings," Theo said glibly.

"Go ahead. Joke about it!" Frank's voice was up a decibel.

"You're the one who lost her job! You're the one whose reputation got shot down! Is that what you wanted? Did it give you something to write about! Let me tell you one thing, today's martyr is tomorrow's old news. Nobody gives a shit!"

"I wasn't fired," Theo said quietly. "I quit."

"What?"

"I said I *quit.*"

"Well, fine! You can play the semantics game all you want, but the fact is you lost your job. A job you loved. So just how do you think you can help anybody now? You sure as hell can't help those kids in East County. So here's a news flash for you. You made a tactical error in judgment, and it cost you the war!"

They were both quiet for a few minutes.

Finally, Frank said, "Thing is, I felt helpless. I couldn't stop what was happening. If you had trusted me enough to talk to me about what you were trying to do, maybe I could have helped. At least I would have certainly been able to let you know when you were being tailed. What possessed you to go to the meetings at the gay and lesbian center anyway? What did that have to do with *anything?*"

"I'm a reporter. I cover town hall meetings as a matter of course. This one just happened to be in Hillcrest at The Center. Besides, I wouldn't have stayed away if Bateman had an army of people following me around. I had a job to do."

"Well, I'm glad that's settled." Frank spat.

He stood up and threw $50 on the table.

"Here's a piece of advice from a cop. Next time you take on a pack of wolves, make damn sure you've got backup."

He turned and walked out of her life. It was less than a heartbeat, less than a blink. Frank was gone, and she knew it would be forever.

Theo sat staring at the folded $50 bill as if it were a divorce decree. She managed to stand up and found that the drinks had taken their toll. She was drunk.

Out on the verandah, she stared down into the murky bay water with its scummy eddies of oil offal swirling opalescent in the fluorescent light overhead.

There's nothing dirtier, she thought. *It's just like deceit and the damage it does. But what is deceit, really?* She had the focused reflection that too much alcohol bestows, so she pondered this.

Is it a means to an end? Or is it the end itself? Is it Lucifer personified or merely a tool? What is old Dickie Bateman, then? She giggled.

If he's the moral guidepost for American Christian values then maybe I am Joan of Arc?

It was easy to hate Bateman for his brand of media hype. He brandished his version of the truth by confusing the issues. When he couldn't discredit the facts, he blasted the messenger. It was a clever ploy. The bad thing is that it worked.

Yep, Theo thought, *that's old Dick. The master slime bag, the epitome of bad poetry in motion.*

At this point, her thoughts seemed to be creating a little motion of their own. A kind of churning eddy started inside her head; it made mental and visual focusing tricky. Theo tried to pay attention to a man hitching his dinghy to the dock. He secured the skiff and headed up the gangplank toward the little bar and nodded as he passed her.

"Looks like a storm tonight," the man said.

Theo nodded and thought the deck felt like it was moving. She steadied herself against the railing. Then, like a choreographed move, she leaned over it and retched violently into the murky water below.

CHAPTER 12

Thankfully, the phone's ringing snapped her back from recounting the painful events of the night when Frank walked out on her. "Hello?"

"Theo, listen." That's how Sam Morley started every conversation. "You do that review yet? I got a deadline here. I could use your help if you're not too busy that is."

Sam was sarcastic. On him it was endearing.

"Yeah, Sam, I'll do it today. I've had some bad news and . . ."

Sam jumped in before she could finish the sentence.

"Bad news? What's happened? You OK?"

"I just found out that a good friend of mine," she paused, "died. I had to ID the body. It was pretty awful."

"Jeezus, Theo. I'm sorry. You sure you're OK?" His concern was genuine.

"Yeah. Yeah, Sam. I'm OK. It's just that with all this going on, I forgot about the restaurant. I'll check it out later today and write something up. I'll email it to you tonight."

"You sure? Maybe you need to skip it. I could just let Ziggy pinch hit on this one." Sam offered.

"Sam, you know Ziggy's idea of gourmet is anything you don't snatch from a drive-thru window. No, I'll do it. Hell, I have to eat, might as well be at Cara Mia's."

"OK," Sam said, "if you're sure. Tomorrow's fine, though."

Typically, Sam never said good-bye, he just hung up. But this time, he was still on the line.

"Sam?"

"Listen," he said, not in his usual brusque voice, "I mean it. You need anything let me know, 'kay?"

"Sure," Theo said, her voice cracking a little. "Thanks, Sam."

Sam Morley was no pushover. He was a tough old news hound, and he was a good friend to those he liked. When Theo left the *Sun* a few months back, his was the only call on her answering machine from anyone in the industry. He offered her a job. She took it. She never regretted it.

*   *   *

Sam Morley hadn't been so easily put off by Theo's scathing humiliation at the hands of Dick Bateman and her subsequent job loss at the *Sun*. Like Theo, he was no stranger to the fickleness of the *Sun*'s upper management.

He'd been a respected columnist at the conservative newspaper for decades. His reputation alone could open any door, and his penchant for jabbing with hard-hitting facts could slam it just as fast. He pulled no punches and in his time, managed to anger public officials, developers, and anyone else he thought abused the public trust. He'd made plenty of enemies both outside and inside the *Sun*.

As it turned out, Sam's firing wasn't over a matter of principal at all; it was a setup, plain and simple.

Sam had come up on the wrong side of one of San Diego's influential kingpins over a questionable housing development in Mission Valley and possible kickbacks to the city council. The developer approached a *Sun* senior executive, offering a fistful of money to silence Sam once and for all. Sam and his boss had never been friends, so this was a chance to shoot Sam down for good.

The executive told Sam about the strong possibility that the newspaper would be sold to an Illinois-based conglomerate. He made it clear that the information was confidential. Sam kept quiet about it, but his boss leaked it to a local TV news reporter who happened to be Sam's friend. When TV satellite trucks pulled up in front of the *Sun*'s Mission Valley headquarters, Sam got blamed.

That same day, he was called on the carpet, and within minutes, he was escorted back to his office by security and observed while he packed up his personal belongings.

When Sam left the newspaper he had helped to build, he had no idea what he'd be doing next.

As Sam tells it now, he drove down to the Little Italy Waterfront Bar & Grill on Kettner Boulevard. After more than a few beers and a real heart-to-heart with the bartender, Sam was convinced that being fired might just be the best thing that could have happened to him.

He decided that what the city needed was a little competition. It was that "epiphany" at Sam's favorite bar that spawned the city's newest rag, the *Waterfront Tattler*. And over the next ten years, the neighborhood weekly grew to become a monitor on the city's pulse.

The *Tattler*, as it was fondly called by its faithful following, was a maverick in the local publishing world. It was a freebie totally supported by ads. Sam figured the price was right and he kept it that way. He filled its pages with freelance articles by journalism students and others. The field was wide open and Sam made sure that the range of topics was varied enough for everyone.

What started as an underground fold-over rag popular in the metro areas of Little Italy, Hillcrest, and the Gaslamp, soon found its way into suburbia. It was everywhere. You'd see it in grocery stores, laundromats, and in local Starbuck's from Santee to Chula Vista and north to Solana Beach. It wasn't gut-wrenching competition for the *Sun*, but it was certainly was a thorn in its side.

With his success, Sam was always on the lookout for good writers. He followed Theo's articles. When she moved into the political arena he figured it wouldn't be long before she stepped on sensitive toes. He wasn't wrong. The day after she was forced out of the *Sun*, he offered her a job, and she took it. He never regretted it. It was a good match.

* * *

It wasn't like Sam to snoop in his employee's private lives, but something in Theo's voice made him uneasy. Call it a newsman's nose, or a good friend's sixth sense, Sam wondered just who had died and how. Having to ID a body at the morgue was something no one should have to do, and it bothered him that Theo had been called in to put a name to the dead. Sam had a gut feeling that something wasn't right, and one thing he never did was to ignore his instincts.

He picked up the phone and dialed an old friend at police headquarters.

CHAPTER 13

"Tommy! Hey, how's it going?" Jarvis Barkley was more charming than usual.

"Oh, hey, Jarvis," Tommy Silver replied in his halting nasal twang. "Man, I was get'n worried. Hadn't heard from you for a while."

Tommy rubbed his hands repeatedly over his hips in a nervous, compulsive way. He was starting to itch. It was a common denominator among addicts when they needed a fix.

Barkley motioned to the rail-thin young man on the street corner, and he slid into the passenger side of the Jag. Barkley slipped the car into gear and eased around the corner to a less conspicuous spot on Sixteenth and Island. He turned off the engine and pulled some papers from the glove compartment.

"Got some good news, Tommy."

Tommy rubbed his lips nervously and smiled.

"*Jeezus*, I hope so. Good news doesn't happen here often."

"Tommy, you look a little tired. You're staying at the mission aren't you? You know I've arranged that with the manager. I want you to have a decent bed and food. I told you I'd take care of the rest of it, but I need to have you safe, especially from the street hoods." Barkley sounded a little worried.

"Yeah, yeah!" Tommy said a little too quickly.

"Sure, I stay there. It's just, you know, I need things." He turned a plaintiff look on Barkley.

"I know, Tommy, listen, I've taken care of you this far haven't I? I'm not going to desert you. I've been getting the bureau to recognize your bloodline. That's what I've been up to." Barkley paused.

"Shit, those bastards. You think they give a damn!" Tommy Silver snorted a skeptical half laugh.

"What do you think this is?" Barkley unfolded a sheaf of papers and pointed to the seal on the last page.

Tommy tried to focus through bleary eyes and finally gave up.

Barkley continued, "It's your *validation*, man! You're in! They've recognized your tribe!" Barkley was smiling.

"Look! There's the seal. I'm telling you the goddamn United States Bureau of Indian Affairs has confirmed the Descansano Indians as a bonafide, validated Native American tribe! Baby, you and your whole goddamn family are *enrolled*!" Barkley waited for that to sink in.

"*Shit!*" Tommy said, a broad smile lightening up his haggard face.

"How the fuck did you pull that off?" Tommy laughed, slapping his knee.

"Tommy, Tommy, *Tommy*, I told you I had connections. Doesn't matter how it happened. Only matters that it did! Now, I need you sign this acceptance page. Once you do that, you become the tribal leader, the *big kahuna*, the *fucking cheese*!" Barkley was grinning, handing Tommy a pen.

Tommy's hand was shaking as he scrawled his signature.

"Hey, don't they have to vote. Isn't the leader voted in?" Tommy asked.

"Not in your case, man. You're blood quantum is high enough, and you're the head of your little family – correction, your little band. That makes you the automatic leader. That's all the bureau cares about."

Tommy handed the pen back to Barkley.

"So when do we build the casino?"

"Well, I'm working on that. I'm working on that, Tommy. You know you can count on me. I'm one paleface that's making up for the years of abuse and neglect. I promised I'd do the right thing by you, and I keep my promises," Barkley said nobly. "I'm a man of my word, Tommy."

The wasted little man's face brightened with trust. His eyes were wet, and he looked every inch the vulnerable, pathetic addict that he was.

"I know, Jarvis. I *know*. You're the only one who cares about me."

"Well, now the bureau cares about you too. They're going to start sending you a check every month. And soon, they're going to grant their approval for your own land. You know what that means, don'cha?"

Tommy nodded excitedly. "Yeah, I'm gonna be one those rich bastards! I'm gonna have my own casino right here in fucking downtown!"

Barkley switched gears. "OK, now, you know you have to keep that quiet. Don't want you talking to your buddies out there on the street. They get wind of this deal, and you're likely to get hurt. Remember what I told you. Keep your mouth shut." Barkley's tone was quietly threatening. The point wasn't missed on Tommy.

"Oh, man, you know me. I don't talk to nobody. No sir, not *nobody*," Tommy said, nervously running his tongue over his lips.

"Good. Good. OK, now," Jarvis said, "you need a few bucks to tide you over?"

Barkley knew that Tommy's crystal methamphetamine addiction always made him needy for cash.

"Wow, man," Tommy laughed anxiously, "you sure know how to reach my inner child!"

Barkley handed Tommy a $100 bill.

"Listen, be careful, Tommy. I mean it. You need to stay at the mission. You can have some fun, but you need to be back at the mission before dark. You got me?"

Tommy nodded. "Yeah. *Yeah,* no problem. I'm there like clockwork."

"OK," Barkley said nodding, "Now, you need a ride somewhere?"

Tommy pondered this, then he thought better of sharing the whereabouts of his best supplier, even with his bankroller. Tommy shoved the bill into his pocket and slid out of the car.

"No, man, *naw*, I'm fine. Gonna get a bite to eat at the Manila Café, then, you know, a little . . ." Tommy laughed as he jerked his hips forward and backward, no explanation needed there.

Jarvis Barkley watched Tommy Silver shuffle down the street. *A little bumpity-bump my ass, Tommy, you're headed for that crack house around the corner.* Jarvis thought.

Well, that's fine, actually, that's better 'n fine. You'll get a good hit and stay low for a few days. In the meantime, that leaves me free to finalize my plan and maybe get my own 'bumpity-bump'!

Jarvis eased the Jag away from the curb and headed west toward Fifth, then north, away from the Gaslamp and into Hillcrest. *I'll just be getting my little bumpity from one of the sweet boys at the new 'health club' on university.*

Barkley smiled thinking about the dark Filipino he'd met the previous night and hoped his excitement wasn't too obvious yet.

CHAPTER 14

The room was private, one of the amenities of this particular club. It was a new addition to the bathhouse scene and catered to those who could spend $500 an hour and had an appetite for the exotic.

It was small and seemed dwarfed by the king-size bed; its black leather headboard reaching nearly to the ceiling made it the clear focal point.

The shower was a dark smoked marble alcove in the bathroom. Ceiling pot lights were recessed in several strategic locations; their soft light cast a golden glow on the polished walls and floor, reflected from the floor to ceiling mirrors, and glinted off the industrial-style pewter fixtures. There was no door, only a half curving wall of transparent glass bricks.

Jarvis Barkley slathered himself lavishly with the creamy soap and continued to run his hands over his buttocks, sliding them down his inner thighs, running them back along his crotch, culminating in long hard pulls on his penis. Every pass over his flesh was charged with electricity and he had to restrain himself from masturbating to conclusion while he waited for his guest.

Jarvis was anxious that his young man hadn't shown up yet and his heightened anticipation was fueled by cocaine and a half-consumed bottle of Chivas Regal.

Jarvis sensed him immediately and turned only slightly to showcase his growing erection.

"I thought you might not get here in time." Jarvis cooed breathlessly, extending his arms in welcome.

"Save it!" The hard staccato of the deep male voice set off Jarvis's sensory alarm, and he snapped around facing the intruder.

"What the hell!" Jarvis was startled and angry at the interruption.

"I told you to meet me later at Bailey's. This is a personal place, and I don't appreciate this invasion of my privacy!"

Juggernaut leaned against the glass brick wall, never taking his eyes off Jarvis, a crooked smile playing at the corners of his mouth.

"You almost have me interested, Barkley, but as you know, I'm not quite your type!"

"Why are you here? Can't you meet me at the club later?" Jarvis shot back.

"Been a change in plans, need to pay a few bills up front, if you know what I mean," said Juggernaut, offering Jarvis a huge white bath sheet.

Jarvis grabbed the towel and wrapped himself, stepping out of the shower, and stomped past the intruder.

"Fine!" Jarvis was extremely irritated and it showed.

"How much do you need?"

Jarvis retrieved a large manila envelope from his briefcase.

"Just what we agreed to," said Juggernaut.

Jarvis tossed the envelope on the bed.

Juggernaut didn't take his eyes off Jarvis, and it started to make him feel uneasy.

"Why don't you just hand it to me like a *gentleman*. I'm not one of your whores, and I don't like to be treated like one," Juggernaut said, with just a slight tinge of menace in his voice.

Jarvis retrieved the envelope and handed it to him. The man's tone had a warning touch to it, and Jarvis was keenly aware that this man was his hired gun and had already killed twice for him. Men who do that kind of job for money have no qualms and no soul. Jarvis considered the critical importance of keeping this man on friendly terms and at a safe distance in a public place in the future.

"I'm sorry if I seemed edgy," Jarvis began in a warmer tone.

"Its just that I'm so damned horny and was really getting prepped, for my *guest*, if you know what I mean."

Juggernaut smiled, showing a gleaming set of perfectly straight teeth. He was extremely handsome, and Jarvis took note of that attribute. It also helped to temper his attitude toward the man.

"You bet I do." He laughed a deep chuckle and started for the door.

"In fact, I'm about to find myself a little R & R tonight, if you know what I mean," Juggernaut said over his shoulder.

He opened the door and was surprised by the slight pretty young Filipino who stared at both Jarvis in his bath towel and the muscular man in the doorway.

"*Hi!* I didn't *know* this was a threesome!" the young man said smiling.

Juggernaut put his hand on his shoulder and smiled.

"Not tonight, I'm afraid, but I have a feeling you two will hit it off just fine without me!"

With that, he gave the young man a friendly shove into the room and shut the door behind them.

Juggernaut was oddly elated. He was on top of his game. *Whether you know it or not, Barkley, now, I'm calling the shots.*

CHAPTER 15

Finding out how Stella died seemed the next logical step. Theo couldn't believe Stella could have committed suicide. She didn't understand why an accident on a boat didn't get reported either.

The answers to these questions lay in the autopsy report. But getting that document at this point in the investigation wouldn't be easy for a layperson. A cop, on the other hand, was a different matter. As disagreeable as that was, it meant she'd have to call Frank.

His office voice mail picked up on the second ring.

"This is Detective Frank Marino. Leave your name and phone number at the beep."

"Frank, it's Theo. We need to talk. You have the number."

She dialed his cell phone and left the same message. Within a few minutes, he called. He didn't waste time with pleasantries.

"Theo, what's wrong?"

"Thanks for getting back to me. Look, I need a favor."

Theo heard the slightly discernable intake of breath on the other end followed by the hesitating, "OK?"

"When will you have the autopsy results on Stella?"

No response.

"Frank?"

"And you need that *because*?"

"Because . . . I just *do!*"

Theo could have bit her tongue. She didn't catch the exasperated retort before it slipped out. She knew if he thought this was anything but the personal plea of a grief-stricken friend he'd shoot her down in a New York minute. She'd have to do better if she was going to get what she wanted.

Frank exhaled a big sigh. It wasn't the response she expected.

"Theo, it doesn't work that way. I know you were her friend. But it takes a family member to get that document and sometimes not even then."

"Look," Frank continued, "If I came on too strong, I'm sorry. I didn't mean to imply that Stella met foul play. I was upset and probably said more than I needed to. I apologize for that. But the fact is, this isn't a criminal investigation, at least not yet. Whatever the coroner's findings, it's the captain that will decide what course of action we take. If it's an accident, then the body will be released to the next of kin. Then the report will be available."

"And if it's not?" She asked.

"If it's not an accident?

"Right. What if its suicide or," Theo hesitated, "something else?"

"Then it's a criminal case. Nothing gets released."

She knew she was losing him. He was starting to sound officious. Theo switched gears.

"Frank? Can you just help me? She is," Theo corrected herself, "*was* my friend. I just want to know what happened. That's all. I'm not asking for clinical details. I guess I just need to know she didn't suffer."

Theo could sense it. She got to him. He didn't let on, but it was how he said, "OK, if there's anything I can release, I'll let you know."

With that, he hung up.

CHAPTER 16

There were just two blocks between Robinson and Washington Streets in Hillcrest. But like nowhere else in the city, this commercial stretch with its hopscotch jumble of trendy curio shops and ethnic bistros was sandwiched between two *Starbucks*.

Abby and Theo sat on the couch in the window of the one at Fifth and Robinson.

They both loved the eclectic nature of Hillcrest. Its weirdness and fun was a love fest between wild adventure and the conventional, a virtual Disneyland for the hip. This morning, though, Theo was gloomy and distracted.

Abby shed her Birkenstock's, crossed her feet on the coffee table, and savored her cappuccino while she scanned the *Wall Street Journal*. Theo stirred her frothy mocha latte and stared blankly at the traffic on the busy corner.

Presently, Abby snickered.

"Can you believe this? It's a list of the late night comics' jokes over Dick Cheney's hunting accident. You know, where he kablamos his 78 year old attorney while they're out hunting quail. Leno says: 'When people found out he shot a lawyer his popularity shot up to 92 percent!'" Abby giggled and read a few more jokes out loud.

Theo managed a feeble distracted laugh, but she couldn't quite muster a full-bore chipping in. She had been watching a homeless woman swaddled in the shabby layers of clothing, worn like the decades of neglect and abuse that lined her face.

The woman shuffled her rusted shopping cart slowly up Fifth Avenue. It was loaded with black trash bags probably filled with cans and bottles. Most likely, she was headed to the recycling center in the Von's parking lot on University Avenue just a few blocks away. Theo thought she was not more than forty-five or fifty but looked eighty.

"It's the street that does that," Abby said, looking over the edge of her paper. "It sucks the life out of them – that and the drugs and alcohol."

Theo nodded. Every time she saw one of the street women, she wondered if that might be her mother. Ridiculous morbid fantasy that it was, she thought it could explain what happened.

When Theo was two, her mother walked away, leaving her with her grandmother. Dena Hunter was never heard from again. The finality of that abandonment left volumes of her mother's own personal history unexplained.

Sometimes, Theo imagined that her mother had been shell-shocked after learning that her husband, Theo's father, had been shot down over the Mekong Delta during that war. Knowing that many of the homeless were vets who'd never been able to dig themselves out of the trauma of Vietnam and its aftermath, Theo thought that her mother could easily have been one of those casualties. For Theo, Dena was as much a war fatality as her father had been.

Theo's depression segued from thoughts of her mother, to her grandmother, then back to Stella. It was like being stuck in a hole of hopelessness with no way out.

"We probably should talk a little," Abby said getting up and heading to the counter for refills.

Talk? That's the last thing I need. Theo thought. Talking right now was about as welcome as a leg cramp. She was talked out and even thinking made her head hurt. What she wanted was mindless visuals.

She contemplated the tight weave of the fabric on the arm of the sofa, then studied the dark wood on the bookcase. It all felt cozy. A safe nook separated by glass from a world that was unpredictable and dangerous.

Abby returned and set the hot mugs on the table. She watched two vivacious "queens" scurry across the intersection, jabbering to each other while sharing a cell phone and gesturing in the air to punctuate their comments.

"Now that's more like it!" she said, turning away from the not uncommon street spectacle.

"Hillcrest – a *fairy*land of enchantment!"

Theo managed a smile and continued to finger the frayed end of upholstery.

Abby said, "By the way, did I say thanks for the use of your car? Well, if not, thanks."

"No problem," Theo said absently.

"I hope this doesn't fall into the same category as three-day-old fish," Abby continued, "but I need another favor. I've got to find something for Connie's birthday. She likes Victoria's Secret's stuff. I thought I'd pick something up at the shop in Fashion Valley mall. Do you think I could borrow it again tonight?"

Theo looked up from the separated seam, which she had managed to make worse.

"Have you ever been to Victoria's Secret?"

"Well, I prefer the sports bras, you know, the ones that strap you down. But I think she likes the push-ups."

Abby cupped her hands under her own breasts and shoved them skyward to make her point.

"Maybe with tassels." Abby rotated them in a circular motion.

"Will you stop!" Theo was laughing now.

"Well, at least I got your attention!" Abby grinned.

CHAPTER 17

"**S**o what's *my* line?" Theo laughed. "Thanks for the *mammories*?"

"Ouch!" Abby winced.

"Uh, nice addition to the décor. Keep that up, and we'll have to buy that piece-of-shit couch!" Abby said, looking at the couch's frayed seam, which was now a two-inch spiked Mohawk of fringe.

Theo glanced down, shocked at her destructive fiddling. As best she could, she stuffed the ragged fabric back into the seam and folded her arms, tucking her hands under her armpits to discourage further textile abuse.

"Seriously," Abby started, "my Beemer's having a major surgical episode."

"And that means *what* exactly?"

"Oh, shit, I don't know, Helmut keeps saying, '*zoon, zoon, Liebling*!'" Abby mimicked her mechanic's German accent.

"*Liebling*?"

"I think it means 'sweetheart.'"

Theo smiled, "He likes you!"

"I wished he liked me enough to put a *rush* on those damn parts for my car! I think they probably ship them by fucking elephants over the Alps! Foreign piece of shit!"

"You love that BMW, and you know it!" Theo smiled, finally relaxing a little.

"Well, I certainly paid enough for it, and I'm still paying! Buying that car was like getting screwed without having an orgasm! Now, what girl, gay, or straight, in her right mind would fall for *that*?"

"You did! Get over it!"

"Sure, easy for you to say," Abby said.

"Your Honda just runs like a Japanese mean machine! Me, on the other hand, I live with the miracle of German engineering and its promise of orgasmic Valhalla, which, I might add, I've yet to truly experience! Go figure!"

They both laughed and then were quiet. Finally Abby broke the silence.

"During your lifetime, you'll need to grieve about a lot of things, Theo. The trick is knowing when you're done."

"I knew it couldn't last." Theo moaned a resigned sigh, "And that means *what* exactly?"

"It means getting on with your life, a big piece of which is dealing with the *Frank* thing." Abby said drawing quotes in the air around *Frank*.

"Oh, God! Here we go again," Theo said exasperated.

"And you think I haven't?"

"Watching you two spar around each other looking for a vulnerable sucker punch would lead me to believe that. Yeah!" Abby said.

"I'm just fine when he's not around. If I didn't have to talk to him face to face, I wouldn't even think about him."

"Well, duh!" Abby rolled her eyes and mimicked her best valley girl retort.

Theo turned away shaking her head.

"This is why I can't talk to you!"

Abby ignored her and continued. "He's not going away, Theo. I can't figure out what he's doing or why, but he's far too interested in you for a guy who's got someone else on his ticket. I never asked you why you two split, but I think now might be a good time to share. I'll bet he's good in bed. Right?"

Theo leaned back and closed her eyes.

"I'm not going there, so quit salivating! It was never the sex anyway. It was far more serious than that."

"That's what you think! Nothing's more serious than bad sex!"

Theo reached for her mocha, took a sip, and studied the floor.

"He said I was too reckless. After the jibes on Bateman's show about me being a lesbian, he was upset. Said that I should stay away from the political meetings and just do what my newspaper said to do. He wanted me to stay out of the battle. He said he was afraid I'd get hurt."

"*Lesbian*," huh? Well imagine! Abby grinned.

"But the part where he was worried about you getting hurt, now that does it!" Abby shook her head in mock disgust. "The *bastard*!"

"Abby, stop. It wasn't a joke then, and its not now. At the time, I was hell bent and determined to fight what was preventing the kids from getting professional help. The 'establishment,' as Frank calls them, was determined to advance their own twisted ideological and political agendas. They didn't give a crap about the kids. I was the only one stepping up to the bat – well, until I got thrown out of the game."

Abby's gaze didn't flinch. "And how's *that* working for you?"

Theo let out another exasperated groan.

"You know, kiddo," Abby continued, ignoring Theo's body language, "you two spar like combatants. All I'm saying is that fighting for peace is a lot like screwing for virginity. It's a no-win battle."

"Abby, come on. We're not 'fighting for peace' as you put it. We're not fighting for anything. We're done. That's all. Just *done*."

"Doesn't look like it," Abby said.

"If you want my take on the whole thing – "

Theo interrupted, "I don't remember asking."

Abby shrugged and went back to her paper.

After an uncomfortable silence, Theo said, "It's just that I don't think he likes who I am. He wants someone different. He wants a stay-at-home wife with kids, someone who cooks and keeps the family in line. Like his mother and grandmother did. He's expecting someone comfortable with the family as a unit with church and christenings and first communions, big Sunday dinners, the whole enchilada. It's what a close Italian family does. It's what his did. He can't see it any other way. I can't do that. I don't know how to be part of that kind of clan."

"Enchilada or lasagna?" Abby smirked.

"Oh, you know what I mean!" Theo blurted.

"OK. Potato – *paw-taw-tow*!" Abby laughed.

Abby went back to the paper. Theo stared out the window.

Presently, Abby looked over the top of her paper.

"Listen, Theo, you were part of a 'clan' as you put it living with your grandmother. She did the whole Sunday dinner thing with Al Stone and those monthly potlucks with the tenants. How's that different from a big family?"

"If you'll remember, Al was her boyfriend and he was married to someone else. And my grandmother never even so much as talked about her past or any of her family if she had any. Hell, she could have been an axe murderer for all I know. It's hardly the same thing as having history that maps out your future. Frank has all that. He has bloodlines and ties with generations of aunts and uncles and cousins. It's who he is. I don't! My work is who I am. It's all I have. Frank doesn't get that. My life is not what he wants his life to be. Bottom line, Frank doesn't want the real *me*."

"You did church on Sundays!"

"Did you hear anything I said?" Theo sighed.

Abby put the paper down. "Yeah, I heard it, and I've heard it all before. First of all, you're not responsible for what your grandmother or your parents did. And as for your job, it's what you *do*, not what you *are*. I think you just accept rejection like it was something you deserved. It's not. Frank was pissed at what happened to you. Guys feel helpless in those situations. You should have let him know what you were up against. You owed him that."

"Spilled milk," Theo said, "it's all spilled milk and there's no sense in crying over it. Not anymore."

"You're right, but you can't keep running away from life. It just keeps catching up."

"I think I'm moving on, not running away."

A tall blond rushed in and ordered a vente nonfat mocha frappucino with extra whipped cream. When she turned to leave she spotted Abby.

"Hey, *Abs*." The blond had a pleasantly surprised tone.

"Cathy!" If Abby looked genuinely taken aback, she quickly recovered. "Hey, back at'cha. How's it going?"

"Can't complain." Cathy smiled. "Haven't seen you around the clubs lately."

"No. I've been pulling extra duty at my place. How's Evie?"

"She's good, I guess. Haven't seen her since we split."

"Sorry to hear that." Abby arched an eyebrow.

Cathy shrugged. "You? Involved?"

Abby smiled and patted Theo's hand. "Yeah, I guess you could say that."

Cathy shot Theo a sideways glance. "Yeah, the good ones always are." She headed for the door. "See you around."

"*See yah*," Abby said a little too clipped.

"*Abs?*" Theo crooned as Cathy dashed out the door.

"Don't ask!"

"Oh, but I must!" Theo whispered amused.

"We were sort of close. Now we're not," Abby said quietly.

"Hmm, looks like there's feelings on both sides if you ask me."

"I'm not asking you," Abby said, feigning disinterest.

"Well, seems to me the alibi has a right to an explanation," Theo said.

Abby picked up the paper. "Nut'n to talk about. Suggest you drop it."

"OK," Theo said, "no *Cathy* confessions and no *Frank* discussions. Agreed?"

"Agreed."

"Movin' on." Theo added.

CHAPTER 18

They pulled up in front of *Las Casitas* just as Frank was climbing out of his car. He waved. Only Abby waved back.

"Hey, Abby," Frank said.

"Hey, yourself, Frank. How's it going?"

"Same as always."

Abby took that for her cue to leave, and she did.

"Theo, I have that information about Stella you wanted."

She was stunned. She ushered him inside and got right to the point.

"What happened?"

"Stella drowned."

"And?"

"And that's it?"

"But how did she get in the slough? She didn't start out there. Both you and the coroner said that she probably was in the ocean first? So how did she get into the ocean?"

Frank said that part would be difficult to know or prove, but that the police were looking into it.

"If I learn anything else, I'll let you know." Then he started for the door.

"But she couldn't have just been swimming in deep water," Theo was saying.

"It couldn't be that simple."

Frank wasn't looking at her. He was done. He was leaving.

"There was water in her lungs. She was alive when she entered the water. There wasn't anything else. That's it," he said again, a staccato clip in his voice.

He had the screen door open when Theo asked if there had been any drugs in her system. There was just the flicker of hesitation, and then he answered "no" without looking at her.

He was out the door, and she followed him.

"Frank, it's too weird. I mean, she had to be on a boat, right? How would she get far enough out to sea to wind up in the slough? She had to fall off a boat. So why wasn't that reported?"

His voice was tight. "They're still investigating, Theo. We'll know *more* when we *know* more."

"What about a copy of the post mortem? Can I get that?"

"No," he said.

"No? You said if there's nothing suspicious the case would be closed. Now, you say they're still investigating. You said that swimming accidents happen all the time. If this was an accidental drowning, why the secrecy? Sounds suspicious to me!"

"Don't put words in my mouth."

He had his car door open and was about to climb in.

"You're lying, Frank!"

He gripped the car door so tight that his knuckles went white.

"Theo," his voice was barely above a whisper but it was menacing hard. "Let this one go. You can't handle it, and I don't want you screwing it up. Plan a decent funeral for her. You owe her that!"

She was still standing at the curb when he peeled away from it.

Theo knew he was lying about the report. That's when she decided that she owed Stella more than a funeral.

"I'll take care of your funeral, Stella." Theo vowed as the screen door slammed behind her. "But first, I'm going to find who did this to you. That's a promise!"

CHAPTER 19

It was late. Theo shed her sleek black cocktail gown and kicked off her strappy sandals. Sam had offered to have someone else cover the assignment, but she figured she just really needed to concentrate on something other than Stella's tragic death. Sam was willing to move her deadline back, but now she needed to get her thoughts down while they were still fresh.

At her computer, Theo started the article on the Brotherhood of Jesus Mission fundraiser. She began.

It was a night of stars, both celestial and earthbound. At the going rate of $2,500 a person, the fabulously wealthy rubbed elbows with Hollywood's glitterati at the Manchester Grand Hyatt. Festivities began at dusk and continued into the night with a private dinner for high rollers who upped the already steep ante. Hard to believe, but it wasn't long before the toney crowd was upstaged. The renowned and wealthy alike jockeyed for position and bellied up to the buffet line that snaked around the room with its never-ending bounty of oysters on the half shell, shrimp so huge they belied their name, and Texas-sized barons of beef. The gastronomical bounty was washed down with $95 dollar-a-bottle Veuve Cliquot champagne that flowed as freely as Perrier on a Frenchman's lips. The opulent affair was a far cry from the excuse for the gala – the derelicts and down-on-their-luck transients who curl up in the doorways and dirty alleys in the mean streets of San Diego.

Theo studied her notes, amazed that she correctly spelled the names of the haute couture designers' duds like Elie Saab, Vera Wang, Versace, or Giorgio Armani that draped the torsos of the women and men guests. She transcribed the names of the great and famous and made her best guesstimate at the evening's take.

Theo fiddled with a few adjectives, typed them in, and then immediately deleted them. She was stuck. Leaning back in her chair, she closed her eyes and stretched, waiting for inspiration.

The evening's most interesting conversation two-stepped around in her head to the tune of a jingle whose title she couldn't remember. It was a silly little ditty she heard in the elevator ride to the hotel garage. It was just a snippet of melody, but it stuck. Somehow, the tune was tied to her final exchange of the evening. It was with the event sponsor – the most fascinating conversation she'd had all night.

The discussion started out innocently enough, but quickly U-turned in a direction she couldn't have finagled even if she'd tried. It went like this.

Theo had slipped outside onto the balcony and was leaning against the stone wall. She sought relief from the stuffy weight of opulence and excess that saturated the evening. In the night air's chill, the self-indulgence of it all was slowly dissipating.

Theo took in the bridge that spanned the inlet of San Diego Bay, disappearing into a park like setting on the Coronado side. A water taxi chugged into the pier loaded with locals and tourists. She remembered picnics with her grandmother on the lawn that stretched along the bay front that skirted the million-dollar condominiums. From a child's perspective, life had been unadulterated and fun then.

"It's an amazing city, don't you think?" It was a rich male voice, solid and confident and slightly slurred.

Jarvis Barkley had taken a similar post against the wall. The smoke from his cigarette curled upward.

"Smoke bother you?"

"No," Theo replied, "I'm probably one of the few people who enjoy second-hand smoke. You get the benefit without the cost!"

She didn't look at him but heard him chuckle.

"Fabulous city," Barkley said.

"Yeah, it is."

"These little soirées ever bore you?" He asked.

"Probably not as much as they bore you!"

Barkley snubbed out his cigarette and finished his drink.

"Well, it *is* for a good cause." He laughed.

"Helping the homeless get off the street is a civilized venture." Theo started. "It's compassionate, only . . . ," she paused.

"Only?" Barkley was looking at her now.

"It's *only* part of it. It's the development that causes some of the problem. Like the one planned in East Village. How can that be good for the city?"

"And *you* know what's good for the city?"

"I don't think destroying neighborhoods is good for anybody. Some of those homes are an important chronicle in history. They are the past. It's who we are."

"Well, I suppose it depends on one's definition of *blight*." Barkley responded, sounding a little peeved.

"One man's blight is another man's front yard." Theo countered.

"And what about the economy? Taking out a few old houses and replacing them with buildings that employ hundreds is good for the city. Instead of struggling with a termite-riddled claptrap, those families will have clean condos and better jobs. It's a win-win."

Theo thought it sounded like a stump speech. It was clear he'd made this argument before.

"That's an old dispute. History refutes it," she said.

"We've seen how a thriving community can be wiped out in the name of progress. Take Little Italy, for instance."

"*Little Italy?*" Barkley laughed, sounding pompous.

"*My dear*, Little Italy is a boom town! There's more commercial enterprise in those few short blocks than almost anywhere else in the city. Upscale eateries and downscale pizzerias – something for everyone. It's energized. It's the *in* place to live. High-rise condos with waterfront views – my god! It's San Francisco South! People live there, they work there, and they play there! It's the new improved micro-community! I'm sorry," he chuckled, "but your argument's bogus!"

It was clear to Theo that Barkley was arrogant, disdainful of any opinion not his own and very, very drunk.

Theo waited before responding. She wanted him to second-guess what she'd say. In oppositional argument, the delay tactic makes the adversary uneasy. She took a moment to scan the view. There was no mistaking San Diego's skyline. The winking lights from its high-rise condos and office buildings, and the waterfront restaurants and shops of Seaport Village lay like a glittering necklace on the deep black velvet bay. It was breathtaking and distant, untouchable. Then it came to her. She knew what to say.

"Where's the blood?" She asked.

"What?" Barkley sounded stunned.

"Where's the *lifeblood* of this city?" Theo said, looking at him.

"When our city fathers sold out to big business, they decided that what this city needed was a crosstown freeway – what we now call the I-5. So they used the 'eminent domain' statutes and took homes and mom-and-pop stores and displaced families and the community. They cut a swath through Little Italy as merciless as Sherman's march to the sea. Little Italy used to be a community. It housed San Diego's mostly Italian and Portuguese families who were the mainstay of San Diego's fishing industry. They married, baptized their kids, and had their funerals at Our Lady of the Rosary Catholic Church. They raised their families in neat little homes with vegetable gardens. Women shared recipes and gossip across backyard fences. And children played stickball in the streets. It was a living breathing place where everyone was connected, either by blood or by friendship. Children felt like they belonged to and were part of the larger family. They were taught to care about this city and its future. It was the stewpot of character building. It was the middle-America of San Diego. You can't put a price tag on morality, Mr. Barkley, in the interest of upscaling economics!"

Barkley smirked, "And how does that have relevance to today?"

"East Village today is no different than Little Italy of yesterday." Theo continued.

"The demographics may be mostly Latino, but just like the Italians and Portuguese families of fifty years ago, they are a community. They deserve better than to have their homes destroyed and their lives uprooted."

"You make a good argument." Barkley actually sounded relieved.

"But you don't see the bigger picture. When Little Italy was developed, that freeway 'swath,' as you put it, ran from the Tijuana border, north to L.A. and beyond. Routing it through the downtown formed a critical link for the entire coastal community. Yes, families were displaced, but they weren't homeless. They simply moved elsewhere. The city, as a whole, benefited. As to the future for East Village, I've already made that argument. You would do well to remember this. Improving anything is not a mistake. It's progress on a grand scale. No city can live in its past forever. History doesn't last. Nothing does."

Jarvis Barkley nodded curtly and walked away. Her dismissal couldn't have been more abrupt than if he'd clicked his heels together and saluted his exit.

At her computer, Theo drummed her fingers on the keyboard. The tune was back in her head and suddenly it clicked.

> Oh, give me land, lots of land under starry skies above, don't fence me in. Let me ride through the wide open country that I love. Don't fence me in.

She hummed the next few bars until she got to the only other lyrics she remembered.

Let me be by myself in the evenin' breeze and listen to the murmur of the cottonwood trees. Send me off forever, but I ask you please, don't fence me in.

Theo Googled the song title. "Cole Porter?" she blurted aloud. "I don't believe it. I figured it was written by Gene Autry or some other cowboy singer. The anthem for preserving wide open spaces, the theme song for the antithesis for the eminent domain model, was written by a city slicker. Imagine!"

She shook her head, "Where's Cole Porter when you need him."

Theo stared at the screen for a while. She was still stuck. What she wanted to say constituted a warning to Jarvis Barkley and those developers who disregarded the lives of others in the name of progress. She wanted to tell them that they had no appreciation for the spirit of freedom. She wanted to scream that they were soulless destructors. Then, she thought about the money that Barkley himself poured into the homeless mission and the money he helped raise that night.

"You might be a pompous ass, Jarvis Barkley," she said, "but at least you're passionate about getting the homeless off the streets. And for that, you deserve an honorable mention."

Theo drummed her fingers on the keyboard. Finally, she typed the last sentence.

"Thanks to the charity of the city's affluent, like hotel magnet and developer Jarvis Barkley, tonight the Brotherhood of Jesus Mission will be able to shelter a few more of the desolate homeless, society's discarded who seek refuge from the pitiless streets. Thank you, Mr. Barkley and those like you, for your generosity and *thieving.*"

"Oops!" Theo chuckled at her typo and corrected the last word to read "*giving.*"

OK, Barkley, she thought, *this time you're off the hook. But in case you don't know it, a wonderful life isn't defined by concrete high rises or industrial enterprise. I hope someday you learn that before it's too late for all of us.*

Theo hit the save button and shut down the computer. It was 1:00 a.m.

CHAPTER 20

The ringing jarred her, and she fumbled for the phone.

"H'lo." Theo's voice was thick and numb with sleep.

"Ms. Hunter?"

Hearing a strange man's voice was a jolt. Theo sat up and reached for the lamp, as if switching it on would identify the caller.

"Ms. Hunter, this is Jack Morris. I'm Stella's brother."

"Stella's *brother*?" She was struggling to climb up out of the confusion.

"Look, sorry about the time, but I work nights and – "

Theo interrupted him. The strength of her own voice surprised her.

"Stella didn't have a brother. I only have one contact, her dad."

"Yeah," Jack Morris said. "If it was *J. Morris*, that would be me. Our dad was *Bob*. Actually, both our parents are dead now. I guess Stella didn't talk much about me, huh?"

Before Theo could respond he added, "Stella and I were all the family that was left."

Theo was still trying to connect the dots. She mumbled a hesitant, "I'm sorry." It felt like stumbling in the dark.

For an uncomfortable moment neither spoke, then he said, "Look, I'm going to be in San Diego in a few days, and I was hoping to stop by to see her place. Would that be OK? I'll pick up her things and pay whatever it is she might owe in rent."

"Sure, OK! I mean, of course you can pick up her things. But there's nothing due. Stella always paid in advance."

"OK, then," Jack Morris said, "I'll call you when I get into town."

He hung up.

Theo was wide awake now. She sat on the edge of her bed, bewildered. She was weighing this new turn of events when the thought occurred to her that she shouldn't just take this guy's word for anything. She wasn't going to release Stella's stuff to some stranger unless he had proof he was who he claimed to be.

In the dining room that doubled as her office, Theo rummaged through the index card file box of her tenant's emergency numbers. Stella's card showed "J. Morris" as next of kin with a Los Angeles phone number. She dialed it. An answering machine clicked on.

"Hey, this is Jack. Leave your name and number at the beep, and I'll call you back."

The voice was the same as her late night caller. Theo hung up. She didn't leave a message.

It was 5:00 a.m. Theo headed into the kitchen when a loud thud on the porch startled her. She peered through the blinds and saw the paperboy heading down the path toward the other units. That's when she realized she was trembling.

"You're just too jumpy! Get a grip!" She hissed at herself.

Theo put on a pot of coffee and retrieved the paper. Standing on her porch, she could just make out the pastel turquoise of Stella's door in the silvery dawn. Until now, she hadn't thought about going in. There was no putting it off.

"Coffee, paper, and then I'll tackle it." Theo tried to plot it out as she closed the door. "The sooner the better."

She shuffled into the kitchen, poured her coffee, and settled into the easy chair, trying not to think about the task that lay ahead.

CHAPTER 21

The key turned in the lock and the front door to Stella's little cottage swung open. Theo took a deep breath and stepped in.

It was just as Stella had left it. A windbreaker slung over a kitchen chair, a water bottle partially full sat waiting.

Theo half expected Stella to step into the room and grab the windbreaker on her way out the door for a run.

Several books were stacked on the table. She flipped open the jackets. They were library books. They were overdue.

A knock on the screen door started her.

"Hi," Abby said. "I saw the door open and hoped it was you. Want some company?"

"Thanks, I'm glad you're here. This is kinda eerie."

"Did you reach her dad?"

"Actually, it was her brother who called *me*. It seems both her parents are dead. He's coming in a few days to get her stuff. That's why I'm here, to pack."

She said this while absently glancing around. She felt like an intruder in someone else's private world.

"A *brother*? Abby looked surprised. "She never said she had a brother."

"He sorta said they were estranged. I guess that happens."

Abby nodded. "Yeah, more than we know."

Abby scanned the room, "Looks like you'll need some more boxes."

"It'll take more than the three cardboard boxes I have. You have any?"

"I can get some from Bailey's. Later this morning, OK?"

"Yeah, thanks. It'll take me that long just pack the kitchen."

Abby barely got out the door when Theo heard voices. It sounded like Oren West, the tenant in unit 4.

Theo hoped Abby would handle Oren. He was one of her favorite people, but she wasn't up to talking right now. She watched the two from behind the curtain. Oren was his usual animated self.

"Hey, Abby, what's going on?" He placed his hands on his hips and tilted his head slightly, "Is Stella back and planning a party? She'd better invite Guy and me or there'll be hell to pay!"

Oren was all about exaggerated emphasis and mock seriousness.

Abby shushed him. She shook her head and put her fingers to her lips. He ignored her.

"Come to think of it," Oren said, "I haven't seen her around lately. Oh, I get it, she's got *company*. Well, probably some gorgeous hunk. I'll just have to see who it is."

Oren started up the steps, but Abby grabbed his arm.

"*Don't* go in."

Even with his hands on his hips like a perturbed queen, Oren was dead serious. It was the *straightest* Abby had ever seen him.

"I knew it! I just *knew* something was wrong. Just yesterday I was telling Guy that something was going on. I could just *feel* it."

This time, Abby's widened eyes and hard stare brought him to an abrupt stop. "Listen! Stella's dead."

He gasped a shocked, "Oh no!" Followed just as quickly with, "What happened?"

"We don't know, Oren. Her body was found in the in the marshes south of Imperial Beach – the Tijuana Slough."

His mouth was open but nothing was coming out.

"It could have been an accidental drowning." Abby paused, lowering her voice, "Or something else. Theo had to identify the body. The police are investigating and, that's all we know. Theo is pretty shook up, and right now, she's got to pack up Stella's stuff. Her brother is picking it up in a few days."

Oren laid a hand on Abby's arm.

"Oh, honey, this is awful. I'm *really* sorry."

From behind the mesh of the screen door, Theo watched. She was touched by the somberness of friends identifying with the tragedy and trying to minimize its impact on her. It was painful and agonizing in a way that stirred up the good things that Stella's memory evoked. She wanted to slip into that safe circle of friendship to join them.

"Hey, Oren."

Theo opened the screen door and stepped out onto the stoop. They both jumped at the sound of her voice. He rushed up the steps and immediately put his arms around her.

"Oh, *hun-ee*, I'm so sorry."

The tenderness in Oren's voice ripped through her, and she started to cry. He just held her and rubbed her back. Theo regained her composure a little and was embarrassed by her emotional outburst.

A pitiful "thanks" was all she could say through her sobs.

Theo pulled the sleeve of her sweatshirt down to cover the heel of her hand and wiped her eyes with it. She mumbled that she had to finish the job and declined Oren's offer of help.

"Maybe we can have coffee later."

"*Absolutely*, sweetie."

Oren looked a little relieved and gave her a quick hug.

"You just call me when you're done, and I'll be right there."

Abby motioned to Oren, and he followed her across the yard, speaking in low conspiratorial whispers.

CHAPTER 22

Theo started in the kitchen. Wrapping the few dishes in newspaper, she began stacking them in the box. She added some glasses, a cheese slicer, spatula, and few other odds and ends. The last two boxes, she filled with pots and pans.

She moved on to the bedroom. Filling most of Stella's clothes into a couple of suitcases she found in the closet, she then arranged knickknacks and odds and ends on the bed for packing in the boxes Abby would bring later.

I wonder what he'll do with this stuff. She was looking at the sad little remnants on the bed. The framed Sea World photo of her with Stella and Abby stared up at her. It was the same one that she had. Her eyes began to water. She turned the photo face down. Grabbing a Kleenex, Theo blew her nose, then added the remaining items from the dresser, some costume jewelry, and a hairbrush and comb to the pile.

The sum of a person's life packed away in a few boxes he'll probably shove into a garage or attic. You put them out of sight until the remembering doesn't hurt anymore.

It was a sobering thought. It led to her thinking about having to rent the place again. She thought about putting an ad in the paper. She made a mental note to have it painted and the carpets cleaned. Nothing else was needed. Stella had been neat. To all appearances, her life had been simple, uncomplicated.

Theo shrugged off the thoughts that would raise more questions than she had answers for. She concentrated on the job she had to do. Amazingly enough, even as hard as this had been, she was making good time. She only had one more room to pack.

*   *   *

The thirties-era pale-green-and-wheat-colored tile was clean, and the bathroom was tidy. She didn't pack the toiletries like the body wash and a pumice foot scrubber; those she placed almost reverently into the small trash can. It felt like desecration. She wondered if she should burn them out of respect. She decided that was impractical.

Theo reached for the toothbrush and toothpaste that were in the built-in swivel compartment on the wall. When she touched it, the whole unit shifted slightly. It was loose. A slight tugging motion and it fell forward, clattering on the tile countertop, revealing a small hollowed-out compartment.

Theo leaned forward and peered inside the small cavity. Something glinted in the dark recess. She switched on the light to get a better look, but the object was small and pushed back at an angle. The thought of spiders and other creepy things made her hesitate, but she held her breath and stuck her fingers into the shadowed hole anyway.

She felt past the crumbled plaster and decades-old dust until she touched the smooth cold object. Wiggling it into a position where she could grip it between her index and middle fingers, she pulled it out. It was a small brass key.

CHAPTER 23

Frank Marino sipped Irish coffee and watched the slim girl maneuver around the vertical bar at center stage to the low bass thumping of *The Doors*'s "Rock Me Baby."

It was only slightly after noon, but the Lion's Lair in Kearny Mesa already had about twenty customers. Several were young marines barely over drinking age. They puppy-dog eyed every move of the young woman on the stage like she was about to toss them a Milk-Bone. They were absolutely devoted, and they were drunk.

There were a few older men hunched over their drinks at the bar. A guy in triple-X-sized Aloha shirt studied a racing form and another in a T-shirt that read, "2nd Amendment – the first homeland security" simultaneously watched the dancer and the game on the big-screen TV.

Angel Martinez came around the end of the bar and motioned to Frank to follow him. Angel's office was cramped and looked like a tornado lived there. A framed and signed Junior Seau football jersey in Chargers' blue and gold hung on the wall behind his chair. A picture of his wife with their two girls sat next to his computer monitor.

Angel motioned for Frank to sit. Angel pulled an envelope from a drawer and tossed it across the desk. Frank fingered the several hundred dollars inside and placed it in his coat pocket.

"Its all there, Frank," Angel said, pouring himself a shot of Chivas. Frank declined the offer of the drink.

"Man, sure do appreciate the job you're doing. Everything's been cool since you're doing the inspections. Gotta tell you, though, things are gonna get a lot easier pretty damn soon!"

"Oh, yeah," said Frank, "how so?"

"Well," Angel lowered his voice, "that's all I can say right now, buddy, but soon, real soon, you'll see, there's gonna be some good things happening for my business."

Frank leaned back in the chair and cocked his head.

"You're so full'a shit, Angel! You don't just throw something like that at me then leave me hanging. What the hell are you talking about?"

Angel shook his head.

"Look, man, I've said more than I should. Just didn't want to hit you with it cold. Just trust me, dude, things'll be a lot easier for both of us. You're a good guy and a hella'va cop. You don't need to be babysitting booty clubs to see if some dancer gets too close to a customer's crotch. Hell, who cares about that shit! This ain't no garden club!

They both laughed.

Frank locked his gaze on Angel.

"You wouldn't be talking about changing the no-touch laws, would ya, old buddy? If you are, then I'd like to know. You got some goddamn inside track I don't know about?"

Angel looked a little nervous. He stood up and edged his way toward the door.

"Dude, just trust me, OK?

Frank got up and leveled his gaze.

"Trust is a two-way street, Angel."

Angel clapped Frank good-naturedly on the back.

"Hey, come on, I gotta go keep an eye on the clientele. Those drunk marines might get crazy on me and fuck up the place. We'll talk later. And, Frank, don't worry! Two-way street, remember!"

CHAPTER 24

The key had a small head with a long shaft. Theo turned it over in her hand and stared in amazement at it. Engraved on one side were five numbers: "81605"; on the other, "Property of U.S. Postal Service."

"Why would Stella hide her post office box key?" Theo whispered aloud.

"Hello?" The familiar voice called out from the bedroom, sending a jolt through her. She slipped the key into her pocket just as Frank Marino walked into the bathroom.

"I saw the door open and wondered if you might be in here," Frank said as his eyes took in the small room, then rested on the chrome toothbrush compartment that lay on the tile counter where it had fallen.

"What's this?" He asked, gesturing to the small wall cavity.

"Oh, I was just cleaning up Stella's personal things, and when I reached for the toothbrush, this fell out. Guess I'll have to putty it up before I rent the unit."

Theo stumbled through the excuse, thinking it sounded less than credible. Frank looked at the cavity then at her. She could tell he was suspicious.

"Seems like a good place to hide jewelry or money."

"Oh? Gee, I hadn't thought of that," Theo said, trying to sound matter-of-fact.

"I guess you're right. I'll have to remember that when I need to hide something of value instead of sticking it in the freezer."

Frank fingered the apparatus while looking at the hole in the wall.

"Find anything in there?" He asked bluntly.

Theo quickly put the toothbrush and toothpaste into the trashcan.

"Hmmm?" She tried to sound casual, "Oh, nope."

Theo thought she'd better grab a quick line of offense.

"So what are you doing here, Frank?"

He was still staring at the gaping hole in the wall. Then he reached into the trashcan and picked up the toothbrush and slid it into a plastic bag he produced from his pocket.

He didn't look at her, he just said, "DNA testing."

His dry investigative tone was chilling. Theo pretended to ignore him and went about clearing out the last of Stella's personal effects. She hoped she looked unruffled.

"Actually," he said, "I thought I'd see if there was anything Stella left in here that might help me wrap this up."

Theo tried to steer him away from the hole in the wall.

"Wrap what up?" she said, readjusting the swivel compartment back into place and wiping down the tile backsplash.

"I thought Stella drowned, an accident. Isn't that what you said?"

"It's still an open case right now." His eyes still focused on the swivel compartment.

"Why do you suppose she didn't tell you about this so you could have it repaired?"

His gaze scrutinized her.

"I have no idea, Frank. Maybe she just forgot."

Theo brushed past him into the bedroom.

"Why are you packing up her stuff?"

"If you must know, her brother asked me to. I'm sending this *stuff* to him. Then I have to get this place ready to rent again. How does that sound, Detective Marino? Make sense?"

"I may need to examine some of her personal effects."

"Well you'd better hurry. And, you'll need a warrant. These boxes and suitcases are going to FedEx tomorrow." She lied.

"That doesn't give me much time." His irritation undisguised.

"Then you'd better get on it!"

Frank moved toward the door. In his best steely voice, he told her not to release any of the items until he'd had a chance to look through them.

"Need a warrant, Frank, shipping these tomorrow."

Frank stopped just as he reached the door. Without looking back, he said, "I'll be back with one. Nothing goes anywhere until *I* release it. Understood?"

Theo ignored him. He punctuated his directive by slamming the screen door behind him.

She quickly packed the last box of personal items and carried it into the living room, placing it on top of the others. Then, Theo looked around one last time and closed the door on unit 2.

CHAPTER 25

Someone was pounding anvils in Theo's head.

She gulped down a couple of Tylenols, slumped onto the couch, and plastered her forehead with a cold towel. She prayed for the Tylenol to kick in and silence the marching band that was quickstepping behind her eyeballs.

It seemed like light years before they began to take effect, but eventually, the dull throbbing subsided. In its place, a wonderful empty feeling started to spread. Into this warm nebulous void, the sound of light tapping on her door intruded.

"Theo," called Oren. "I brought *goodies.*"

She let out a low moan and wished she'd had the foresight to install a trap door on the porch. This was no time for a coffee klatch, but Oren wouldn't be ignored.

Cracking the door slightly, Theo hoped her green death mask of pain would banish him. It didn't work.

"Oh, *sweetie!*" His shock was genuine as was everything about him. "You are in real need of a friend-fix!"

He brushed by her taking charge of her kitchen like Harriet Nelson or Beaver Cleaver's mom.

"And since Abby's not around, *I'll* just have to do."

The thing you had to love about Oren was that he would not be put off. Like a doting mother hen, he just did the right thing whether you liked it or not. Theo heaved a big sigh and crumbled onto the couch. Within a few magic moments, the aroma of the freshly brewed coffee filled the room. When he brought her a mug, she held it to her head.

"Don't say another word, honey." He began, "I know this must be so hard for you, and I just want you to know that we're here for you."

This he said while ripping open a pouch of kitty treats, which he dribbled lovingly into KC's bowl. The cat curled around his legs, purring like a boat motor. KC liked Oren almost as much as catnip. Like KC, Theo had taken to Oren West and his partner Guy Hamilton the moment she'd laid eyes on them.

They'd just gotten to town from somewhere in the Midwest and were staying in a weekly rental down on Pacific Highway. Her ad in the *Tattler* brought them to her door. They said they'd "just fallen in love" with the place at first glance and begged her to rent to them. She did without even checking their references. Theo just trusted her instinct. This time she was right.

Oren was a set designer at the Old Globe Theatre in Balboa Park; Guy, a pastry chef at the elegant U.S. Grant Grill downtown. Where Guy was charming in a reticent, shy way, Oren was his opposite. Along with Oren's many talents, he was also a shameless gossip. He managed to know more about everyone of Theo's tenants than she had discovered in their months or years of residence or association.

For example, Oren knew that Dottie in unit 5 was an adept marijuana farmer, growing a healthy stash, which she supplied to the elderly Mr. Shovitz in unit 6 to help him through the difficult chemotherapy he was undergoing after recent prostate surgery.

When Oren shared this bit of information, Theo acted astonished. However, knowing Dottie's penchant for the unconventional, she was not surprised. Dottie's affinity for the agrarian lifestyle was part of her charm as was her beading, sewing her own clothes – particularly tie-dyed skirts and blouses – her staunch vegetarianism, membership in several ecological organizations, serving as a docent at the Natural History Museum, and her unconditional devotion to fighting the establishment and bucking the current political hierarchy – whoever they were.

"So I just couldn't help wondering, Theo," Oren was saying as he opened the pink bakery box of cream-filled éclairs, "how something so awful could happen to that sweet thing. I mean, how'd she wind up in the *Tijuana Slough* for God's sake? What the hell is that anyway?"

Theo was only half listening and mumbled that a slough was just another name for an estuary where fresh water and sea water meet. She was about to say that estuaries were important feeding and breeding grounds for all kinds of fish and sea life, but before she could, Oren was rambling on.

"I mean, who names anything spelled like *slough* then pronounces it like *slew*"?

His eyes opened up like saucers and he immediately clasped his hand over his mouth and whispered, "Oh my God, isn't that ironic?"

"Well," Theo stuttered, but thought there was no point and just closed her eyes pretending not to listen. Oren immediately launched a different direction and offered her an éclair. She greened up like the wicked witch of the East and declined. Oren frowned slightly, muttered that Guy had just made them that morning, and made some reference to casting pearls before swine. Then, he helped himself to the larger of the two.

"Whatever you call it, that's a big stretch of no-man's land for a party girl. She wasn't smuggling illegals or dope was she?"

"Why would you think she'd be smuggling anything?" Theo managed, turning her head to avoid the aroma of the pastry. At the moment anything edible was as appealing as ripe fish.

"Well, I'll just bet it had something to do with that boyfriend."

"What boyfriend?"

"Why the *mobster*, of course!" he said, sucking out the creamy custard.

CHAPTER 26

Her jerked head turn was met with an instant migraine reminder to sit still. Theo winced as a sharp jab ricocheted off the side of her skull.

"What are you talking about?" She all but hissed through the pain.

Oren gave her a haughty sneer over the rim of his tortoise shell Fendi hornrim glasses, loudly sucked the last of the cream from his finger then punctuated his irritation by dabbing the corners of his mouth with a napkin.

"Listen, sweetie, you've got to tone down some of that *'tude* or you'll pop every vein in your head!"

Within seconds, he retrieved her Imitrex prescription from the cupboard and stood over her with a glass of water and two pills cradled in the top of the lid. Theo gratefully swallowed the meds and drank most of the water. Next, he placed a hot damp towel on her forehead. Within minutes, the pain subsided.

"Better?" Oren asked while he reached for the last pastry.

"I don't want to preach, sweetie, but didn't I tell you to keep your serotonin levels up? It helps keep those migraines at bay especially when you're under a lot of stress. And listen, *Ms. Peachness*, if anyone's been under stress," he paused, "well, enough said! I'm just going to bring you a nice turkey sandwich later. That tryptophan works wonders on those serotonin levels and kicks depression's butt!"

Theo was finally able to focus on Oren's face without feeling like she was being broadsided by a freight train. She took a sip of the coffee he'd brought her earlier and managed a pathetic little smile.

"*Baby*, I'm not saying you look awful, but if you're seeing a light at the end of the tunnel, just walk toward it!"

Theo actually snickered and was thankful it didn't hurt.

"You saying I look like death?"

"Warmed over and toasted!" Oren laughed.

"OK, now that I can actually process what you're saying," Theo began, "so what makes you think Stella was seeing someone let alone a 'mobster' boyfriend."

Oren's smile was deliciously wicked, "*Well,*" he began, "Dottie and I were planting the poppies and daylillies just along the path. By the way, don't you think they turned out lovely?"

Theo didn't even have to verbalize irritation this time. Her look could have melted mud.

"OK, *OK*," he exaggerated fear while reaching for the last éclair.

"Well, Dottie and I were planting those beautiful orange poppies and sunny yellow daylilies that so compliment the rustic charm of the garden, and yes, *you're welcome*! That's when we overheard her arguing with someone. We just *knew* it was a man. She was saying that she didn't like how things were going. Oh, and something about betraying a trust. Then she said that she didn't think she could do it."

"Do *what?*"

"We couldn't tell *what*. But whatever it was it really got to her. She started to cry. No, sob, actually. We both wanted to go to her but figured we should just leave her alone."

"Did you or Dottie find out anything else?"

"Well, Dottie had an appointment, but I went back about an hour later but she was gone. That was the last I saw of her."

Theo interrupted, "Why do you say he was a mobster?"

"Well, you remember when Guy and I first moved here?" Theo nodded despite the dull throb at the base of her skull that had started to creep back.

"Go on."

"We told you how we were saving our money so we could get into one of those cute little condos in *Little Italy*. Not that we don't love it here, honey," Oren placed his hand on Theo's arm in apology, "it's just that we hoped to make an investment that provides a return and . . . ."

Theo cut him off, "Oren, *please*."

"*Honey,*" Oren said disapprovingly, "you're going to bring that sucker back on if you don't keep a lid on it!"

He motioned for her lie down and knelt behind the arm of the sofa and began to gently massage her temples.

"You know you can't live on that Imitrex stuff, it will just rot your stomach. All you need is a bleeding ulcer!"

She let him ease away the pain.

"How's that?"

"Much better," Theo mumbled, grateful for the void where the throbbing had been.

"OK," Oren said, "*Now*, where was I? Oh yes. Well, Guy was picking up odd jobs doing catering on the side, to earn more money you understand. Anyway, he was catering this lavish party at this very fancy penthouse condo downtown, you know, those million-dollar beauties off Columbia Street, the ones with the harbor views. Well, there were these guys who looked like Vegas-types, big flashy jewelry and $5,000 suits. Boy, Guy said they could use a serious makeover from a real queer eye! It just goes to show that all that Mr. Toad's money can't snatch you some style, honey!" He laughed at his own joke.

"And there were these girls. Guy said they were hookers, but they weren't the run-of-the-mill girls you find down on the streets or in the bars, these gals were like models with style. They had to be pricey, Guy said. Anyway, so Guy's bringing in the appetizers when he sees Stella. At least he thinks it's her. He says he can't be sure because he had to get something from the kitchen, and when he came back into the room, she was gone. He figured she either left or went into a bedroom with one of those Vegas bozos."

The Stella Oren was painting didn't jive with the one Theo knew. Besides, what Theo knew about her relationship with Councilman Delaney didn't fit into a party girl's scenario.

"Oren," Theo began, "Stella didn't live a lavish lifestyle. She was a secretary for an environmental political consultant. Other than her day job, she pretty much spent her time here. I don't even think she dated." Theo lied.

"Just what 'environmental organization' do you think she worked for?" Oren said cynically.

"Honey, there isn't an environmental agency in this city that Dottie doesn't have a connection to or with. And she said she *never, ever,* saw Stella at any of those offices. So I don't think 'environmental' was exactly the 'organization' our Stella was connected with. If she was, then, *damn,* if I'm not every girl's hot dream!"

"Oren, what you're saying is that Stella worked as a prostitute! I can't accept that." She wasn't expecting a response.

"I knew that girl. She didn't entertain Las Vegas businessmen or any other businessmen for that matter!"

Oren gave her a long sideways glance. "Well, OK. But I only know what Guy said he *saw.*"

"Yes, but he wasn't sure." Theo pushed.

"Guy doesn't say much, but he doesn't miss a thing either. If he said he thought the girl in that penthouse looked like Stella, I'd bet my Gucci loafers that it *was.* That's all *I'm* saying."

A throb started again. Theo felt sick and a little dizzy. The prospect that the Stella she thought she knew and the one that was unfolding before her eyes were one and the same was sucking the air right out of her. If anything Oren was saying was true, then Stella's life was a nightmare of deception. Theo felt her own life was unraveling. She just wanted to be alone.

"Oh, damn!"

"Sweetie, what's wrong?"

"Oren, I forgot I'm on a deadline. I have to review this new restaurant."

"What place is it?"

"*Cara Mia*. Heard of it?"

"Guy may know something about it. I'll give him a call. I might save you a trip if he's got an inside line. What do you need?"

"Well, the menu for starters. But I'm supposed to eat there. If I try to eat anything I think I'll just puke."

"Listen, I'll go for you. I'm a real *foodie*. In fact, next to Guy, critiquing *anything* is my favorite pastime!"

"Oh, Oren, if you could do that for me, I'll personally treat you and Guy to dinner."

"*You're* not cooking are you, sweetie?" He feigned a look of horror.

"I'll take you *out* to dinner."

Oren smacked his lips in mock delight.

"Well, let's just see if we can get any scuttlebutt, shall we? Then we'll negotiate payment!"

Theo hugged him. He hugged her back and held her quietly for a few minutes.

"You'll get over this, Theo, it just takes time. We'll be here for you. You don't have to go it alone."

Theo felt her face flush and tears well up. She brushed at them slightly embarrassed. Out of habit, she choked back the feeling with humor.

"Thanks for trying to cheer me up. Next time I'll eat my own éclair. I promise."

He flashed his charming smile, said he'd hold her to it, then he slipped out the door.

Theo fell back onto the couch and snuggled under a soft chenille throw. She pulled the coverlet over her eyes to shield them from the light and tried to banish thoughts of Stella from her mind. It wasn't long before she was asleep.

CHAPTER 27

Theo awoke with a jolt and startled KC who was stretched along side her on the couch. The cat gave her an annoyed glance, then stood, stretched, extending one leg behind him, leapt down, and strolled toward the kitchen.

Although it was nearly 8:00 p.m., gray bars of light streaked the back of the couch in the late twilight of daylight savings time.

Theo squinted through the blinds at Stella's unit. A light breeze fluttered the flowers in the hanging baskets. She remembered the day Stella brought them home from the nursery.

Just then, the screen door bobbed on its hinges as if it were opening. Theo half expected Stella to step out onto the porch with a watering can. She tried to choke back the tears, but they had already started. She cried for Stella, for her deserted flowers, and for herself. Desertion, like truth, is a reality that's best faced squarely, and Theo understood that drill better than most.

A yowl from the kitchen saved her. It was KC's complaint that his bowl was empty. She fed the cat then stepped into the shower. The hot spray on her head and at the base of her skull further relaxed her muscles, adding to the fuzzy relief and banishing the remnants of the migraine. She thought about going to bed but decided she wanted to be outside in the fresh air.

She pulled on jeans and a T-shirt, grabbed her zippered hooded sweatshirt, and headed out the door in the direction of Bailey's. Just before she did though, she slipped Stella's key into her pocket.

CHAPTER 28

B ailey's was situated on Fifth Avenue in Hillcrest nestled between an architect's office and a salsa dance studio. It fit in well with the Hillcrest persona.

Like every other establishment on the Hill, Bailey's was a crossover – a popular haunt for its gay and straight regulars alike. Its décor was fifties men's club – deep red leather booths, dark wood wainscoting, and soft lighting courtesy of amber tinted craftsman-style glass wall sconces.

It was a relaxing place to have a drink and a nosh, hash over the latest political topic with a friend or stranger, or just relax without big-screen TV's blaring from four walls.

Abby was the working partner at Bailey's and was tending bar when Theo got there. Theo settled into one of the back booths – a clear signal that she needed to talk. Abby served Scotch and sodas to two well-dressed middle-age men who were politely arguing the pros and cons of the impending California gubernatorial recall election.

Abby smiled and sidestepped the request for her opinion on the matter. "Well, if you're asking me who in the field of thirty-five candidates I'd vote for, I can only say you've got the option of voting for a bad politician or a bad actor. Seems to me we've done both before."

The two sneered with good-humored disdain. She left them arguing.

Abby slipped into the booth and slid a coffee mug across the table to Theo.

"You OK?"

Theo stared at her coffee like it was a Magic 8-Ball with all the answers. "Yeah. I will be. It just takes time."

"Yeah, time and study," Abby said.

It was Theo's Grandma Julia's mantra. They both recited in unison: "Time to heal and study to get your mind off it and onto something else."

Abby was pleased to see Theo smile.

"Ya know kiddo, that whole 'healing time' maxim is true. Losing Stella like we did was a terrible bad thing. You take the time to accept that it is, then you let yourself heal."

"You should go into the psych-healing business, Doc," Theo said.

"I almost did, remember. I like this one better." Abby smiled.

"I get to 'wax wise' with the clientele and then there's those tips!" Abby mockingly rubbed her thumb and index finger together.

"Abby," Theo started, "did Oren tell you anything about Stella that surprised you?"

"Like what?"

"Like she might not have been who we thought she was?"

Abby leaned back in the booth and leveled her gaze over the rim of her glasses. "No. Should he have?"

"Oh, I don't know," Theo sounded exasperated, "He told me some things that he suspected about her, like maybe she didn't work for an environmental agency and maybe she had a mob boyfriend."

"Theo, this is *not* HBO, and we're not *The Sopranos*. No one has a *mob* boyfriend these days!"

"Oren and Guy think Stella did. And maybe Dottie too!"

"Mother-earth Dottie? Get *out*!"

"That's what he said."

Three lawyers seated themselves at the bar and spied Abby.

"Hey, Abby, how's about a round here, we're celebrating!"

Abby nodded and smiled back. She shot Theo a stay-where-you're-put look and headed toward the bar.

CHAPTER 29

Abby was still high-fiving and trying to unsnarl herself from the lawyers' party when Connie Tominsky slid into the seat opposite Theo. "Hi ya!"

"Hey, Connie," Theo was surprised and pleased, "they let you off early tonight?"

Connie was Abby's current love interest. She was a graduate student at the University of California and waitressed part time at the Lion's Lair in Kearny Mesa.

"They called too many of us in tonight and asked for a volunteer to leave. I said, 'hey, I'm your man' so to speak! So here I am!"

Abby waved from the bar. Connie motioned for a Coke, naked with no ice or booze. "I'd love a rum and Coke, but I've got a research paper due Friday," she explained, "so I'm just going to hang out here and work on it until Abby closes."

Connie pulled out her laptop and rearranged the table. She was rifling through her papers and found an envelope.

"Oh, shit! I forgot to mail this. Theo, you have a stamp?"

Theo fished around in her wallet and produced a half-empty book.

"Sure, how many you need?"

"Just one. I was supposed to mail this last week. My boss asked me about it tonight. So of course I lied and said I had. But I'd better make an honest woman of myself."

Connie wrinkled her nose and beamed the innocence of a kid at the top of her game. She was twenty-eight but looked sixteen. She could have been the poster child for ingénue of the month – short-cropped blond hair and saucer eyes as aqua blue as a swimming pool. Theo couldn't imagine anyone, let alone Connie's boss, giving this bright-eyed Kewpie Doll a hard time about anything.

Connie was smart in a nerdy way, and in her naiveté, she thought she was invincible. Which – no surprise – was the very reason both Theo and Abby worried about her working at the Lion's Lair. To their credit, they'd tried to channel her into something less sleazy. Connie assured them both that the bouncer kept a good eye on the clientele; plus, she said that the tips alone paid her tuition, and the night schedule didn't interfere with her day classes and laboratory work.

"Geeze, guys," Connie argued, "I can't make that kind'a money slinging burgers at Micky D's!"

Fact was that many of the girls that worked the strip club circuit were college students like Connie. Tuition and living expenses were the very reasons they danced or waited tables. In truth, they were safe, mostly. The typical customers were young servicemen, barely over the legal drinking age limit themselves. This wasn't surprising given that San Diego was home to the Navy's Ninth Fleet, as well as base to the Marine Corps Air Station at Miramar, the Marine Corps Recruit Depot near Point Loma, and Camp Pendleton in Oceanside.

At any given time, San Diego County housed the largest concentration of military might in the continental United States and most of it just barely twenty-one. So it made good "skin-club" business sense that the bars proliferated throughout the county with many in close proximity to the military bases.

Connie, like her contemporaries, had the self-assurance of youth and the confidence in her own immortality. She passionately argued her case thusly, "Most of those guys are so plowed after a couple of drinks that they couldn't do more than just *look* even if they wanted to! And you've seen Mano. As Samoan bouncers go, he's King Kong! He can lug two burly jarheads out, toss 'em in a cab, and they'd think they'd been tucked in for the night!"

Connie made it sound as harmless as taking gate tickets at Sea World. Of course she was the only one of the three that believed it. As far as Theo and Abby were concerned, the jury was still out on that one.

Theo glanced at the envelope and saw it was addressed to *Friends of Chuck Feldspar.*

"So your boss supports Feldspar? His campaign got down and dirty about strip clubs and bars being too close to schools. Why would Angel put money into *his* campaign fund?"

"I dunno." Connie shrugged.

"Angel gave each of us girls $300 and told us to donate $250 to Feldspar. We just had to write our own checks. I *totally* forgot, but I guess its OK to send money even after the election."

Theo was processing this when Abby joined them. She settled into the booth, kissed Connie on the cheek, and fingered the five-pound textbook on the table.

"Hi, babe, what's this? Homework?"

Abby glanced at the computer screen and announced the title like it was boiled liver: "The Molecular Aspects of Viral Replication and Host Cell Interactions"? Abby shivered. Theo winced like she'd just gotten a whiff of a bad smell.

"OK, you guys," Connie chided, "don't act dense! You'll thank me some day when I take the Nobel for finding a cure for cancer! In the meantime, I need to work on this for my lab tomorrow? So a little R-E-S-P-E-C-T, please!"

"Hey," Abby replied, "in that case, carry on Madame Curie or should I say Aretha!"

Theo was staring at the envelope on the table. She waited for the friendly sparring to subside, then she said, "Abby, Connie's boss gave her money to send to Chuck Feldspar's campaign fund. He had all the girls at the strip club do it. Doesn't this seem just a little *off* to you?"

Abby raised an eyebrow, looking bewildered.

"And that's because?"

Connie went back to writing the check.

"That's *because* Feldspar claimed to be antibars and strip clubs. He ran his campaign on it."

"Maybe he changed his mind."

"Come *on*," Theo pushed, "it looks fishy."

Abby and Connie cat-eyed each other and snickered in unison. "No, she didn't say it *'looks fishy'*!" Abby was still grinning.

Connie stuffed the check into an envelope, licked, and sealed it.

"*I* don't see what the fuss is about. Angel gave us money for a donation, plus a bonus, all we did was give part of it to Feldspar. So what? Angel's got kids in Catholic school. Maybe he just feels guilty about running a skin joint. Maybe supporting a holier-than-thou politician is his penance. I'm not about his motives. All I know is that he gave us an extra fifty bucks for our effort. I could use the money. Besides, just seems like politics as usual to me!"

"I'm just saying," Theo started.

Abby saw where Theo was going with this. She gave her a just-drop-it look. Theo ignored her. Theo was mounting her soapbox. Connie scrunched up her forehead and started to pout.

Abby, trying to avoid careening toward a three-way crash, attempted to shade the glare on the obvious.

"Sure it looks suspicious and maybe it is. This stuff goes on all the time, Theo. It's not new. Running a campaign takes big bucks, even a city council seat. It's one of the lowest on the political food chain, but it can cost the candidates over $200,000 a piece. What regular guy can afford that? Could you? I couldn't. I'd be surprised if the big donors *didn't* come up with schemes to get around the rules."

"Abby," Theo persisted, "It's *illegal* for Connie and the other girls to take money from their boss and write campaign checks to Feldspar's campaign. What they're doing is dodging campaign financing laws. The law limits the amount a single donor can contribute to a candidate without the public knowing who's financing the guy and how much he's getting from them."

"I know," Abby started, "it speaks of some under-the-table deal. But you don't think this is anything new do you?"

Theo was exasperated. "It's about thumbing your nose at the rules. It's not a gray area. It's black-and-white campaign fraud!" Her voice went up a decibel.

Connie fidgeted and shot Abby a get-me-out'a-this look.

Theo kept going.

"What's the payback for the strip club? Feldspar is anticlubs. He campaigned on it. Does Angel supporting this guy make any sense to you? This screams fraud! It's a big deal, don't act like its not!" She ratcheted up another decibel.

Connie jumped in, pleading at this point.

"Honest, Theo, I *have* to do this. Angel gave me the money and expects me to. I can't just give it back to him and say, 'Sorry, my friend says this is like *so* wrong!' How well do you think that'd go over? I'd probably lose my job, and regardless of what you think about the business, it's a job I need right now!"

Connie's eyes brimmed up like flooded blue lagoons and spilled over. She unceremoniously wiped them on her sleeve.

Theo was about to make another point when Abby applied a slight vice-like pressure on her arm.

"Theo, you're right. But I don't think Connie can go back on her word to Angel. And I'll just bet you *get* that. This is a little far down the road for her to hang a U-turn now. Besides, it's not up to Connie or us to take Angel on over this. And who really cares, anyway? It's not my concern whether Angel's a hypocritical bastard or a sleaze just trying to cozy up to a crooked politician."

Abby held up the envelope.

"*This* – is a *regular* bag of french fries compared to the *super-sized* stuff that goes on all the time. Feldspar's going to need a lot more money than a few $250 donations from the working girls to pay off his campaign debts. I'll bet he's into a few developers' pockets too. It's all one big shady-deal lovefest. It's not going to change anytime soon, Theo."

Abby stuck the envelope in her pocket.

"It's OK, Connie. I'll put it out for tomorrow's pick up."

Abby dropped her head slightly and eyed Theo over the top of her wire-rimmed glasses, "We'll just forget about it, right?"

Theo nodded like she'd just been told to go to her room.

* * *

Around 11:00 p.m. Theo left the club. With all that was going on, she didn't get a chance to talk to Abby about Stella's key.

Quickstepping the distance between Bailey's and home, Theo mulled over the Feldspar campaign donation. She decided to talk to Abby privately about it the next day. She could smell the front-page headlines and saw Connie and the other girls heading for jail time at Las Colinas Women's Prison if a federal attorney caught wind of it.

So absorbed had Theo been with the whole campaign financing issue that when she fished around her pocket for her door key, she realized it was the first time in days that she'd been fixated on something other than Stella. *Maybe I'm just moving on.* She thought with a twinge of guilt. *Or maybe I'm revving up for something bigger.*

CHAPTER 30

The "email waiting light" was blinking on Theo's computer when she settled in around 11:00 p.m. She scanned through them all and clicked on the one from babycakesisa10@networld.com; it was from Oren.

"Well, here we are doing your homework for you, Ms. Priss, and you can't even invite us over for coffee. We'll talk about your lack of hospitality over dinner at some pricy restaurant later! Right now, here's what you need to know about *Cara Mia*."

Theo scanned Oren's evisceration of the new restaurant. She almost had to reach for her asthma inhaler.

"For all its pseudo-Tuscan-wanna-be style" is how he began, "Cara Mia claims to be Little Italy's newest Italian Bistro, but honestly, the place screams heart attack villa smeared on a crostini!"

Oren didn't stop there. He proclaimed the fettuccini overdone and called it pasta *al dentures*. He then went on to describe one of the main entrées as "topped with an indescribable pasty white sauce that bore the name *Alfredo* but tasted like cowboy gravy. The creator of this abomination should be handcuffed and boiled in this outrage!"

Oren was relentless, slicing through everything from antipasto to dessert, separating pretense from the bone with the skill of a seasoned butcher.

Finally, he proclaimed the restaurant's gastronomical fare as "deserving of the *bite-me* onion award for its array of repulsive offerings of refuse erroneously labeled *Cuisine of Tuscany*."

Oren's bitter critique of the restaurant's décor was surgery bordering on disembowelment. He pounced on it sparing no details. Oren called it a "fake garden of cheap silk plants, furnished with plastic-molded chairs reminiscent of a trailer park rummage sale or a tailgate party at an *Oakland Raiders'* game." Then he capped it: "One can only hope that the cuisine-a-la-tailgate surpasses the fetid offerings of this Little Italy's newest trattoria wannabe that can only be described as a cloudy rhinestone among the dazzle of the area's crown jewels!"

Theo sat stunned. It was far better than anything she could have written and nasty enough for the *New York Times!* She couldn't recall ever seeing anything so eviscerating in a local paper or anything this side of the Rocky Mountains. She loved it!

Polishing Oren's prose only slightly, she created a nom de plume – the "Gauche Gourmet" – then noted that this was but the first offering from the fresh new food critic, Oren West!

Theo was satisfied that she more than met her obligation to Sam. Without a second thought, she typed her T. L. Hunter byline and hit the send key.

CHAPTER 31

8*1605* etched on the keyhead and the words *U.S. Postal Service* stared back at Theo like a taunt.

"Almost a lead, but not quite." She mumbled.

Having the key without knowing where the box was located would be a tough code to break. There were literally hundreds of post office branches throughout the county, and since postal boxes, like the mail, are federally protected, Theo figured calling a branch to ask where the box was located would just raise suspicions. Second-guessing Stella was the only open option at the moment.

The logical move would have been for Stella to choose a post office closest to home. That would be the one on Cleveland Avenue in Hillcrest. That was reasonable, of course, but, as Theo was finding out like so many other parts of Stella's life, not exactly a slam dunk.

Theo considered that Stella might have selected a branch near her job. *And that would be – where?* She thought, now bewildered by the copious possibilities and lack of straight facts. She chewed her thumbnail and winced, disgusted with herself for slipping back into that bad habit.

"Maybe I could just look in the yellow pages under Escort Service for Mobsters." Theo grumbled and immediately felt a twang of remorse that hit like a quick slap. It wasn't in Theo's character to be disloyal to a friend and feeling like she had been would gnaw at her like an ulcer.

Theo reminded herself that regardless of whatever secret life Stella might have led, the memory of Stella-the-friend deserved respect. And if anything, delaying judgment until she had all the details was certainly warranted. Too bad the facts on hand were about as solid as fog. Where Stella worked, what she did, who she was – these had become the blurred areas, the bits of the puzzle whose shapes kept morphing into something else. Right now, none of the pieces fit. It was a struggle to make any sense of it all. Trying to piece together the fragments of Stella's life was more than a challenge – it was as compelling as a dare – and that was something Theo was a complete sucker for.

It was just like to Theo to pick up the gauntlet tossed at her feet and rally back. Its how she approached all life's injustices, with fervor and dedication, especially if malice or cruelty were involved.

In school, it had been her battle against the "in" crowd – the girls who seemed to have everything Theo didn't have a clue about – the looks, the clothes, and all the right moves. They taunted her for being different; she fought back. They ridiculed her bookish style; she read more. They criticized her as being too studious; she worked harder. They called her weird; she dressed to prove it.

As much as she outwardly protested their self-absorbed mediocrity and smallness, Theo secretly hoped she could win them over, convert the harassers into supporting sisters who could embrace a common cause for good. Eventually, realism would set in, and she was forced to accept that she could not transform anyone other than herself.

Once she had given up hope of ever converting them, she was free to decide how to deflect the nasty snipes and barbs that the spoiled prigs shot at her, her friends, and the others that might be outside the in crowd's prized circle. The hurtful salvos launched with no more intention but to embarrass and denigrate were cruel and clear evidence that they were callous about other people's feelings. They were mean. Seeing that for the damaging spiteful destructive force that it was helped Theo immensely. It was the rich soil for the seed that grew into Theo's championing of causes – lost or otherwise.

Regardless of what it later became, in the heart of an idealistic preteen, one-upmanship became the tantalizing goal, the badge of courage, the sacred challenge. Theo aimed high and threw herself into the battle like a courageous Joan of Arc. Of course, she had a willing cohort in Abby.

The *Bitch Barbies* is what Theo and Abby tagged them, and they lived up to their name. They were vicious to anyone not in their clique. Abby was better at ignoring them than Theo was. But the constant wheedling eventually took its toll, and Theo found herself on the short end of resistance. One day, she just snapped. Had she given it more thought she definitely would have reconsidered. What happened was pretty juvenile and could have ended a lot worse than it began.

It was at the end-of-year sixth grade swimming pool party. She had been splashing around in the shallow end, perfecting her dog paddle. Abby was somewhere off in the deep end with her snorkel, looking like she knew what to do with it.

The Bitch Barbies were giggling and splashing each other to delighted squeals when one of them spied Theo's fledgling efforts. Soon the whole group was laughing and yelling that she should get a "duckie" inner tube and play in the kiddy pool. It was a mean taunt, and Theo should have ignored it. Ordinarily, she would have; this was just not one of those times.

One thing led to another, and Theo was goaded into jumping into the deep end. She didn't even consider the fact that she couldn't swim. It was one of those rare moments when the folly of youth ignores the logic of reasonable outcomes and scoffs at the laws of physics.

Theo poised herself on the side of the pool trying to emulate what she'd seen the other girls do. She figured she did OK in the shallow end and would just do the same in the deep side.

"How hard can it be," she reasoned, knowing that two things were certain – first, she'd go under, then, she'd rise up to the top. She figured once she resurfaced, she could dog-paddle safely to the side – piece of cake.

In the heat of the moment and with the classmates egging her on, Theo leaned over the side, bent her knees, pointed her fingers toward the water, and arched forward in a curved lunge. She hit the water hard and even though her form wasn't all that bad, it was skewed enough to go wrong.

The complication came with the impact and the strain on her bathing suit strap. Slamming the water stressed the S-hook on the strap that held up the front of her suit. It snapped on contact and her own body's downward propulsion stripped the upper part of her suit away from her torso like peeling a banana. In a panic, Theo grabbed the strap, and struggling against the forces around her, she tried to pull it back up.

Some might argue that her insistence on holding on to a scrap of fabric when she desperately needed to use both arms to paddle upward was an indication of how quickly the slow-wittedness associated with hypoxia can hit the brain in a drowning situation. Her actions didn't make any sense. But anyone who knows how susceptible preteen girls are to peer pressure can understand that saving face by protecting her nakedness was Theo's only thought. She could not let anyone, particularly the Bitch Barbie tormentors, see her dilemma. Releasing the strap was simply not an option, no matter the consequences.

With only one arm free to propel her upward, Theo made about as much headway as a rock. She began to sink downward toward the bottom of the pool. Now, the terror gripped her. She panicked, she gulped water, she was confused, she forgot to kick her legs. She was going under, and she would drown. She knew it, and terrifyingly enough, she accepted it.

In an instant, Abby was there. She pushed Theo's butt upward until she broke water then guided her to the side of the pool. It was over. She was saved.

At her computer, Theo pressed her temples bewildered with a slight twinge of panic that the feelings from a twenty-year-old incident could come flooding back with the almost sickening freshness as if it were yesterday.

She tried to analyze it. *Of all the stupid things, what triggered that memory recall? It wasn't about not fitting in at school, and it wasn't about barreling ahead in a fit of anger without thought of the consequences. It wasn't even about how lucky I was that Abby saved my butt, literally.*

Then, it came to her. In those few moments when she thought she'd die, Theo didn't care any more about the mean girls or their taunts or even how red-mad fury had taken hold of her and propelled her into a stupid and dangerous act.

In those few precious moments with the pressure building in her ears and her chest collapsing, the crush of thousands of gallons of water pressing her downward, and the face of death looming over her, what she remembered clearly was the overwhelming sense of sadness at losing her own life and the pain of not seeing her grandmother ever again. It was excruciating, unbearable.

And that's what she felt now – the guilt of letting herself be goaded into a foolish action that blinded her judgment and boomeranged a knockout punch right between the eyes. That's what trapped her – the mantel of self-condemnation for her own foolishness is what paralyzed her then. It was guilt that she wrapped around her neck like a boa constrictor and what would have dragged her to the bottom of the pool.

She thought about Stella. *Is that what happened Stella? Was the guilt of your double life what pulled you down? Was the fear of exposure worth dying for?*

Theo considered how jagged fragments of life can come at you and how impossible it is to put them together so you can get the big picture before you do something stupid and irreversible. Fear of exposure, anger, retaliation – all primal forces – they can be lifesaving, or they can end badly.

"What you needed, dear friend, was an Abby to jump in and save your butt." Theo muttered.

She fingered the key, considering all the reasons why she shouldn't get involved any further let alone even try to locate the right post office branch. She ticked off the impossibilities and impediments. She considered her already overburdened schedule.

Theo had every reason to just toss the key in the trash and get on with her own life. She really didn't need the complication, and yet there were those nagging questions about Stella, and not to be cliché, she had a key.

"Oh, what the hell!" She grumbled.

Theo grabbed the phone book and began leafing through the pages under the listings for the United States Postal Service. She scanned through columns and columns that seemed to multiply with her effort. Finally, squinty eyesore from scrutinizing the small print, she decided there really were only five possibilities.

She already had jotted down the Hillcrest Branch, next was downtown on E Street across from the main library, another in Mission Valley not far from the Fashion Valley Shopping Mall, and the last was on Midway Drive.

Theo hadn't considered the Midway branch at first, but she'd been there several times and thought that its immensity alone might have been a draw for Stella if she was aiming for anonymity. The place was monstrous with a veritable maze of mailbox corridors packed in tighter than a warehouse of sardines.

"That's it!" Theo felt a punch of excitement. "That'll be my first try" – she eyed the 11:30 p.m. readout her computer screen – "first thing in the morning."

CHAPTER 32

Theo fidgeted. She fixed some herbal tea. She munched caramel popcorn flavored rice cakes. She drummed her fingers on the desk. She stretched. She checked her email – a Target ad and her daily horoscope:

"Travel, study, and spiritual issues could all be in the spotlight for you today. Open your mind to some new ideas right now, and you will profit from the investment. If you find yourself presented with an unexpected challenge, remain flexible. The twig that bends in the wind will live to face another day."

"Huh?" she muttered. "Remember 'grasshopper, the twig that bends in the wind . . ?? Nice! Who writes this crap! Jackie Chan!"

The clock blinked 12:30. She was still wide awake. She closed down her email and stared at the screensaver photo on her desktop. It was a Monument Valley red rock formation stuck on a stark royal blue sky. Looking like another planet its other worldly aspect was usually calming, just not now.

"OK," she mumbled, "plan of attack. If I hit the Midway branch at around 5:00 a.m., I should be able to be in and out before it gets busy."

This made sense. She figured she'd do a quick reconnaissance and get out before drawing attention to herself and arousing suspicion. It was now 1:00 a.m.

But, she reasoned, that's a big place. *It may take longer to check the boxes than I think. Getting there around 4:00 a.m. improves my chances exponentially.* It was now1:15.

On the other hand, she continued, chipping away at the now greatly modified plan, *2:00 a.m. would certainly give me enough time and assure even greater privacy.*

Theo considered the downside – a lone woman prowling around the empty corridors long before dawn – it was something to think about. She did for about ten minutes, then, *Hey, that branch is open all night!* Theo reasoned. *There must be security guards and night shift workers, even an occasional patron.*

Despite the risks, she latched onto this idea like Velcro, convincing herself that not raising undue suspicions might be smart, even brilliant. Telling herself that she was edging closer to her target time, she managed to rationalize herself out the door.

Soon, the taillights of Theo's Honda were streaking west on Washington Street, crossing the railroad tracks at Pacific Highway, passing the skateboard park nested beneath the I-5 overpass, veering left onto Barnett, then a sharp right onto Midway Drive.

Easing into the empty parking lot, she pulled into the first space closest to the stairs. With the engine off, Theo sat in her car for a few minutes and debated going in.

The monolithic concrete structure was as imposing as a prison only without the security of guard posts. It was forbidding, deserted. Theo swallowed her apprehension and reminded herself that the reason she was there in the wee hours was to avoid suspicion. It was simply the best time for what she had to do. She fumbled in her glove compartment for the heavy flashlight which she thought might help in her search but could also be a handy weapon if needed.

Moments later she was rounding the outside wall of the open-air terrace where row upon row of metal post office boxes stood sentry. Oddly enough, it reminded her of the urn reliquaries entombed in the Wall of Remembrance at Holy Cross Cemetery. Theo shrugged off a shiver and started scanning the addresses on the boxes.

The numbers began with *370,000* and continued downward. She scouted the rest of the terrace corridors, but it soon became clear that the number sequence she was looking for wasn't in the terrace. She continued past the bronze plaque proclaiming that the building was situated on Dutch Flats and noted it to be the very spot where Charles A. Lindberg and his *Spirit of St. Louis* departed on May 10, 1927, on his history-making flight to Paris. She felt a spark of encouragement at the notion that Lindberg's extraordinary success might just be an omen prophesizing her own. *I can only hope!*

Theo headed toward the double doors and was startled as they slid open automatically. Once inside, she moved noiselessly past the express window where she was comforted by the occasional voice of an employee from somewhere in the deep recesses that stretched beyond the barred window and the rumble of the mammoth mail carts being wheeled in for processing.

At the first row of mailboxes, she caught her breath as the *809* sequence began. *This is it!* She thought excited, *now to find the right section.* Theo moved quickly from corridor to corridor, scanning section by section. She had just finished searching the fourth wall when, amazingly, there it was – *81599, 81600.* Theo repeated to herself.

She trembled now, holding the flashlight in both hands trying to calm the staccato of light that pulsed, strobelike off the wall of bronze and glass stretching for what seemed like miles of passageways. Then, Theo caught her breath as the light glinted on *81601.* She skipped it quickly down the sequence of numbers *81602, 03, 04,* then, as if she was the moth and it the flame, box 81605 glowed in the stuttering beam of light, Plymouth Rock-solid – as if it had been calmly waiting, expecting her.

In the dark with the beam of her flashlight trembling on its face, Mailbox 81605 awaited. Theo hesitated only a split second, savoring her shock and delight, then she slipped the key into the lock and turned.

The resulting *click* echoed in the dim corridor, and she was sure anyone within a ten-yard radius heard it. She felt a twinge of fear and jerked the door more as a reflex. It swung open revealing a large manila envelope – nothing more. Theo grabbed it, relocked the door, then she bolted for the exit.

Making her way through the maze of dimly lit passageways, the only sound was her excited breathing and the *squeegee, squeak* of her running shoes on the polished concrete floor.

Outside, she bounded toward her car, clicked the automatic door unlock, and was saluted by her car lights flashing in response. Theo slid behind the wheel. She fumbled with her key and realized her hand was shaking. Jabbing at the ignition, she missed, and the key slipped from her fingers and fell to the floor. Straining to see in the dark, she scratched around on the floorboard. She was rewarded with a gum wrapper, a damp wad of leaves, then her fingers grazed the hard metal of the key. Just as she raised her head, she was startled by a face peering in her car window. He was so close his breath fogged the glass.

Theo let out a frightened yelp. Without taking her eyes off the man at the window, she punched the automatic door locks with her left hand while her right felt for the ignition slot. She found it in a miraculous millisecond, and the key slid in. The Honda's engine sputtered, coughed, then settled into a steady hum with no hint of the thunder that her heart was pumping out at what felt like two hundred beats per minute. She slammed it into reverse and squealed backward.

"Hey, lady?" the disheveled man yelled.

"Geeze – no call for rudeness."

The man jumped back from the careening car. For all her fluster, he remained calm with all the acceptance of a person who lives with rejection and expects it. The derelict clutched a shabby blanket around his shoulders and shuffled off muttering, "Probably don't have no cigarette let alone a light, anyway." The man vanished into the dark as quickly as he appeared.

Theo slammed the gearshift into drive and peeled out of the parking lot and on to Midway Drive. She barreled through the intersection just as the amber light turned red.

Theo didn't stop shaking until she was back in her cottage, secure behind her own locked door.

CHAPTER 33

Theo stared at the envelope. It was addressed to Stella Morris, but the return address was her own!

Stella wanted me to have this! It was the flash, the obvious truth – Stella's stamp of approval – something Theo needed. Still, she couldn't bring herself to start. The chilling fact was that she got it. She felt it as glaring and as hard as an icy stare. Theo had to decide whether or not she was willing to accept the consequences of delving into that secret world, that life where the *other* Stella lived – and died.

She could feel the mental clock ticking away the seconds like it was tuned into a heartbeat. Her gut was telling her that where this was leading could be ugly. In the end, she accepted it on the face of trust.

"If this was what you want me to know, Stella, there must be a damn good reason."

Theo ripped off the tape and slipped the contents out onto her desk: several typewritten papers, wadded more than folded, and a rose-colored suede bound journal. She unfolded the typed sheets. Each sheet had columns of names. Each had a different heading – the name of a city council member. One sheet for each of five out of the eight council members: Chuck Feldspar, Bradford Thomas, Lori Fischer, Mario Sanchez, and Ted Delaney.

Theo stared at the lists but couldn't concentrate. She knew there was some significance to the papers or Stella wouldn't have gone to the trouble of saving them, but they weren't the prize. She tossed them aside and picked up the journal.

The notation inside the flyleaf simply read: *"My Thoughts."*

I have always kept a journal. It began. If I hadn't burned them after filling the last page of each one, I guess I'd have thirty or forty by now! Why keep them when some memories are too painful to remember? If I die, I don't want anyone to know the things I've done. When I see them go up in smoke, I feel new . . . reborn . . . some might call it 'purification' . . . I call it a 'fresh start.' I'll probably burn this one too when I'm done. But for now, here goes:

Day 1: A new day! This is the first day of my new life in San Diego. San Diego! I LOVE this town! The weather is like being on vacation every day! I've got this great place – a darling little cottage – like I've always dreamed about! It's cozy! When I look out the window, I see the most beautiful garden with a fountain and mountains of flowers, no ugly brick buildings with bars on the windows like L.A. I'm close to Hillcrest with restaurants and bookstores and shopping! It's like living in Disneyland!

Day 5: Met Abby, Theo's friend. I feel like I've known these girls forever. Last night we shared a big bottle of champagne. Theo said we were celebrating my new place and my new job! We laughed and joked and polished off that bottle, then staggered out to Mo's on university for one of the best hamburgers I've ever tasted! Theo is like a sister (at least what I think a sister would be like), and Abby is just like a big brother . . . well, she is gay!

Day 23: Juggie called. He was pissed at me, scolded me for taking too long to get to work. He's right, of course. Just one time I wanted to be different. I knew my heaven on earth wouldn't last long. Well, I guess I've played 'vacation' long enough – now its back to my real job!

Day 25: Bobby G. Lots of fun! Not at all like TD. At least Bobby likes to party. Too bad I can't just spend time with him. Shit! Juggie is pushing for commitment from TD. The others are way ahead of me – so far. TD is tough. He doesn't want sex like most guys – just likes to talk. Must be gay! Need a different approach! I'd better get hot, or I'll be on Juggie's shit list and that's nowhere I want to be!

Day 40: The girls were such fun today. I felt like a kid. For once, I'm liked for me, not for what I can do. Imagine hanging out with girls with no sex and no cameras rolling! It's a first for me! God, don't let Juggie find out! He thinks I've wasted enough time already!

Theo made quick notes: *"hanging with the girls with no sex and no cameras."* Meaning what? And who the hell is Juggie?

*Day 45: I can't believe what's happening . . . how did I get so involved with TD? Last night, he made love to me! It was real . . . not just a "romp" after a porno flick . . . this was **REALLY** honest! It frightened me. He took me in his arms and held me and told he'd help me. He said I needed to get out of the business or I'd get hurt this time. He wants us to go out of town so we can spend the whole weekend together.*

"Business!" Theo blurted out – it was a statement, not a question. She was hearing Oren's words as if he were sitting beside her.

"And there were these girls . . . hookers . . . not the . . . girls you find down on the streets . . . these gals were like models with style."

"And one of them is Stella." Theo added.

Theo slammed the journal down and walked into the kitchen. She poured herself a small glass of *Johnnie Walker* and swallowed half in one gulp. It burned all the way down her throat and stared a coughing binge that left her throat sufficiently raw. She threw herself on the couch and held the pillow over her face waiting for the throbbing to subside.

When she could focus on something other than her burning throat, she considered the facts: (1) *Stella's own words are clear; she was in the business of gaining men's trust any way she could. She was messing with politicians;* and (2) *someone named Juggie told her what to do, so that makes him her . . . what? . . . PIMP?*

Associating the word with Stella was disgusting, it left a residue like curdled milk – she wanted to rinse out her mouth. She took another swig of the scotch. The second went down easier.

Theo eyed the journal like it was the guilty party standing before a judge waiting for the sentence. It was the confession she didn't want to hear.

"Where's the sweet kid? The one who giggled at silly jokes, lived to shop, cried at old movies on TV, and played Scrabble like she wrote the *Merriam-Webster*. I don't want to know this other Stella. The scheming world-weary woman with men notched on her belt like some gun-slinging whore."

Theo didn't want to continue reading. She reached for the remote and switched on the TV. It was a *Dr. Phil* rerun. He was interviewing guys who cheat on their mates.

One guest was opining about his love for his wife and five kids, but explaining how he just liked to be with a woman who didn't look tired or complain about the house and kids and bills. The audience was booing.

This is stupid, she thought, *his excuse makes perfect sense – not that I agreed with it – but it really makes sense to him.*

He said that he was having a hard time at work – he was in sales. His boss was on him every day to increase the profit numbers. He said he came home hoping to hear his wife say that he mattered to her, but all he got was complaints.

The wife countered with how tough it was to pay the mounting bills, keep the kids in check, and how miserable she felt when she looked in the mirror and saw she weighed twenty more pounds than she wanted to and had age lines that made her look and feel like her mother. She said she wished he'd just say "I love you" instead of "what's for dinner" when he walked through the door.

The show was in turmoil – everyone picking sides. Theo felt sorry for the husband *and* the wife. Theo wondered: *How do you fix your miserable life when it's so much easier to just step out of the picture for few hours?*

Then, an amazing thing happened. The husband walked over to the wife, knelt on both knees, and begged her forgiveness. He said he didn't see the twenty excess pounds. All he saw was the beautiful woman he married. He said all he wanted was to feel like the stud he felt like when she said "I do" and that he just wanted to know that she still loved him and didn't think less of him because he wasn't the millionaire he said he'd be when he proposed to her. So they cried and embraced.

The crowd exploded with applause and Dr. Phil acted like he'd just pulled off a millennial treaty between Palestine and Israel. Theo switched off the TV.

"OK," she mumbled, "so you've got to walk ten miles in someone else's shoes to get where they're coming from? Yeah, I get it, *I get it.*"

She glanced over at the journal. It lay open on the desk, a penitent waiting for an invitation to come forward to receive absolution – hers. Her gut said she should bundle it up and burn it like Stella said she did with all her previous journals.

Theo wanted to stop while she still had good memories of Stella. She didn't want the burden of knowing about this dual side to Stella's life. She was willing to forget what she'd learned that night – it was more than enough – she just wanted to close the door on it – to put it to rest.

Why, then, she thought, *am I struggling with this? It's simple – or should be.*

The thing Theo couldn't avoid was the clear logic of why she had possession of the journal in the first place. The answer was solid as stone and it posed the questions she had been trying to ignore: *If Stella wanted it destroyed, wouldn't she have done it herself? Why then did she send it to me? She was willing to expose her other life to me – what did she want me to know?*

So, Stella was a working girl – in the oldest sense of the word. She was still my friend and she want's me to know something – something she couldn't tell me while she was alive.

That was the hurdle Theo needed to get around – she had come to terms with the obstacle that prevented her from concentrating on the real issue – which was the question that begged an answer: *What was Juggie's game? And why did Stella change the plan?*

Theo picked it up and started – again.

CHAPTER 34

Day 50: *Las Vegas was nothing like it's ever been for me! We stayed at the Mirage, a small suite, not the big presidential apartments I've been in before when Juggie was pulling the strings, but a nice, lovely room – just made for us! TD didn't gamble or hang out in bars or flirt with anyone! He was there . . . the whole time, just . . . for me! We had breakfast in bed every day! We stayed in the room until night – not just making love although that was more times than I can count – we talked and told silly jokes and talked some more. Can this really be real? I feel weak inside when we're together. I ache when we're apart. What is this painful thing? Maybe it's an ulcer . . . or maybe It's love (?).*

Day 53: *Back in San Diego, I can't believe it hurts so much to be separated from him. This can't be love. I can't let this be love . . .*

Day 55: *I needed a break. The girls and I went to SeaWorld today. For a few hours, I forgot about the mess I'm in. The best part – I got splashed! It was a setup, and I knew it! I went along with it for them – but really, it was for me! I had so much fun. I felt like a kid. Funny I don't think I really know what being a kid is. Juggie was my world for so long that I can't remember ever having times like I had today. Being with Theo and Abby is like living a fairytale. For once, I wasn't just looking at a happy family through a picture window – this time I was in it! I belonged! I came so close to telling them everything, but I know better. I'm the alien here, the Martian, the square peg. I don't belong no matter how much I want to. Thank God I didn't say a thing. I kept my cool. I can't ever let* *them know who and what I really am. That way, they just might like me a little longer.*

Taped to the page was a ticket stub to SeaWorld and a concessions receipt for a Diet Coke and fries.

Theo felt the hot sting of tears, and she mixed it with guilt for good measure.

How could I have been so blind? How did I miss those signs? Oh, Stella, the past is the past. It's not the future! Where you've been is old news; it's where you're headed that matters! I would have helped you . . . if only you had trusted me! If only.

Theo's insides ached, and she felt somewhere between emotionally decimated and physically hung out to dry. Her eyelids grated like sandpaper. She was beyond exhausted.

She eyed the clock – it was 4:00 a.m. It seemed like time was suspended. "This must be the longest night of the year! I can't believe all that happened in the span of just a few hours!"

Snuggled up on the couch with the soft afghan pulled up to her chin, Theo finally slept.

CHAPTER 35

Theo wondered why a motorcycle was revving so close to her ear so she turned her head to muffle the noise. Finally, a very irritated KC nibbled her earlobe.

"KC!" Theo yelped.

The cat, satisfied that he achieved his purpose, immediately moved to plan B. He thudded to the floor, lumbered over to the door, and began a strident scratching tirade.

Theo mumbled a death threat but dutifully stumbled to the door as any well-trained cat owner would; the cat made a hasty escape. Just as she latched the door, something glinting in the direction of Stella's unit caught her eye. Then, she saw it again – a light flickered in the left front window.

Theo shifted her view to see if might be a reflection from the light post in the center of the courtyard. Altering her viewpoint didn't make it reappear. She started to turn away almost convinced that's all it was. Just then a quick darting light flickered in the window to the right of Stella's front door, appearing then disappearing. Whatever it was moved from room to room.

Icy panic inched up her spine. She fumbled for the phone but couldn't find it in the dark. What happened next made sense only in the kind of rush that propels one into combat. In retrospect, Theo wouldn't have taken the chance. Naturally, hindsight would come later.

She slipped out her back door into the alley. Using bushes for cover, Theo crept alongside the building in the shadows until she was out of range of unit 2's front windows, then she dashed across the front pathway and into the shrubs and crouched under the bedroom side window. Cautiously, she peered in.

The circular beam was tracing along the wall and over the boxes that were on the bed. Theo ducked as the light moved in her direction. She could hear movement, footsteps, and then it was quiet.

Suddenly, the back door creaked open, and a man stepped out onto the stoop. The door closed quietly behind him, locking automatically. She crouched back into her cover. The figure turned and looked directly at the bushes where she hid. Theo didn't breathe and hoped her heart's pounding didn't betray her. Her eyes strained to see some feature of the burglar so that she could pick him out in a lineup. As he passed in front of the bush, he turned his face just slightly; he was listening. Then, apparently satisfied that he hadn't been seen, he stepped into the faint shaft of streetlight. Theo had just a glimpse. She bit her lip as Frank Marino slipped behind the unit and headed toward the street.

Theo didn't move until she heard the car drive away. Her chest was beginning to constrict, and she felt cold and clammy. She made her way back to her own cottage; triple locked the door and found her way to the couch. Tucking her knees up under her chin, she pulled her over-sized sweatshirt down to her ankles.

Theo faced the window, eyes fixed across the courtyard at unit 2 and rocked slightly back forth. It was a nervous response mechanism she hadn't used since childhood.

Since Stella's death, Theo's world had been one confusing blur. Nothing seemed as it had been. Stella wasn't who Theo thought she was. Frank was mysteriously hiding the truth about Stella's death, and now, he had broken into her cottage. Then there was the damning journal.

Frank was right about one thing, she thought, *I'm in over my head and sinking fast. This bad dream just keeps morphing into one ugly scenario after another.*

She sat there mesmerized, watching Stella's cottage.

Her phone's ringing startled her. She grabbed at it and whispered, "Hello?"

"Ms. Hunter? This is Jack. Jack Morris."

"Yes, Mr. Morris." Theo's voice was little shaky.

"Sorry for the early call," Jack Morris said, "but I'm here in San Diego. Could I stop by later this morning? I need to talk to you."

Theo glanced at the clock. It was now almost 5:00 a.m.

"I'm up," she said, "Now's fine."

"Thanks." Jack Morris said, sounding relieved. "I'm just down the street. I'll be right there."

The coffee pot beeped the end of its brewing cycle just when someone rapped lightly on her door.

CHAPTER 36

Jack Morris was nothing Theo expected. He was tall, muscular, and had brown hair with blond streaks that curled softly down his neck and rested on his collar. He wasn't just ruggedly handsome; he was sculpted like one of those male models in the Calvin Klein ads. His jaw was square and solid, and his deep blue eyes were warm, yet serious. He was as drop-dead handsome as Stella had been gorgeous.

"Theo? I'm Jack." He said, extending his hand.

"Hello, Mr. Morris. Please come in."

She gestured toward the couch and said she'd get the coffee. He didn't sit. He offered to help. Her small kitchen placed them closer to each other than she would have liked. Finding herself only a few feet from him added to her awkwardness. After pouring two steaming mugs, she was relieved when he settled on the couch. She grabbed the club chair opposite, allowing a comfortable distance between them.

"I know you didn't expect me like this." He began. "But I haven't been able to sleep ever since the police called about Stella, and I haven't stopped pacing since I got the autopsy report. I thought if I could just see her place. I might be able to figure out what she had gotten herself into. So I came here. Does that make any sense to you?"

Theo thought that nothing had made any sense for quite a while.

"Of course, Jack, er, Mr. Morris," she said.

"Please," he said, "I'd feel more comfortable if you called me Jack."

Theo smiled a small self-conscious smile.

"I understand. You must feel so *helpless*."

The moment the word left her lips she wished she could have jerked it back – reminding the dead girl's brother that he was "helpless" in the face of his loss made Theo feel like she slapped him across the face with a sympathy card. She bit her bottom lip and started to apologize. He waved it off.

"I know what you meant, and you're right. I am helpless. She's gone and under the worst possible circumstances. Not knowing how it all came about is torturing me!"

Theo placed her hand over his.

"I'm so sorry, Jack. It's hard to understand how a good swimmer could just drown like that."

He looked at Theo as if she lost her mind.

"She wasn't good enough to overcome the alcohol and drugs she took! No one's that good!"

Theo was stunned.

"Alcohol I can understand, Jack. But drugs? What kind of drugs?"

"Ecstasy, cocaine, and meth, plus the booze!" He angrily spat the words.

"I don't believe that, Jack."

Theo never trusted Frank's bland version of the autopsy report, but Jack's story was too appalling to accept.

"Believe it?" His voice rising angrily, "I don't want to believe it either. But it's hard to argue with the coroner's report. She had enough drugs in her system to kill her. That's what the report said. She had cardiac arrest. They didn't find any water in her lungs."

"So that meant she didn't drown." Theo finished his sentence.

"*Drown?* Hell no she didn't drown!" He was pacing now.

"She was dead when she hit that water. That's the only consolation I have. Maybe she never knew what happened." He looked away from her, lost in his own thoughts.

"I thought I knew her. I guess I was wrong. Drugs! I just can't believe she'd do drugs."

"Jack, I knew Stella too. I can't believe she'd do them either. It just wasn't like her."

He walked to the window. She let the silence calm the air between them. Then, "Jack, did you keep that report?"

He didn't flinch. "I started to burn it," he said his back still to her. "But then, I just couldn't."

He turned away from the window. His frown was pinched and painful. "It's not something you want to keep, but it's all I have right now."

She stood up and placed her hand on his arm.

"Jack, have you seen her yet?"

He shook his head. "No. I thought if I put it off, it meant that it didn't happen. But she was ID'd by friends, and well, I have that report. I guess there's no question anymore."

He looked directly at her.

"Were you one of the friends?"

Theo swallowed hard. Her throat felt like a rock had lodged in it.

"Yes." She managed to whisper. "I was one of them."

"How? I mean, was she badly . . . ?" He didn't finish.

"We were able to identify her, Jack. It *is* Stella."

He set his mug on the table and walked to the door.

"I want you to see that report," he said. "It's in my truck."

The news that Stella was on drugs was one more crushing blow. It just didn't jive with what Theo knew about her. But then, since she began reading the journal, nothing made much sense – not anymore.

CHAPTER 37

Anyone who's ever seen one knows the coroner's report is a brief scientific analysis of every possible body part and organ, including the brain.

In clinical terms, it's a cold and graphic schematic of slicing up a once living human being. This one was no different.

Theo plowed through the medical diagram. Her emotions were seesawing between revulsion and morbid fascination.

The report revealed that Stella had enough ecstasy mixed with cocaine and methamphetamine in her system to cause hemiparesis, a stroke that resulted in a paralysis that affected the right half of her body. As if that weren't bad enough, she had also ingested alcohol. That lethal cocktail was enough to bring on the cardiac arrest, and that, according to the pathologist, is what caused her death.

Theo thought that maybe Stella was at a party and took the drugs or someone slipped them to her in drinks. A few days ago, Theo wouldn't have believed any of this. Even now, with the facts slapping her in the face – she still couldn't. Her gut told her that Stella was not a habitual user. What would prove or disprove that theory was the toxicology tests on brain tissue.

Theo was no expert, but she had done some research on ecstasy while writing an article about the RAVE phenomenon. She had interviewed kids that had been to RAVES – those parties, often held in clandestine locations, where high-energy techno music was loud, repetitive, and pulsated – the perfect backdrop for the wild gyrating crowd who downed an assortment of designer drugs like they were M&M's. Ecstasy was the drug that was a common denominator in the dangerous equation.

As more and more young people began to show signs of the dangerous side effects of these freely shared, mind-bending drugs, law enforcement, parents, and school authorities marshaled forces to cut off the kids' access to the stuff. For some, their efforts were too little too late.

The damage suffered by the heavy users of ecstasy was long-term and irreversible. Tests revealed that over time, the drug caused nerve cell damage to the brain, and that's what Theo was looking for in Stella's report. That would tell her whether or not Stella was a long-term user.

Regardless of whether or not there was evidence of habitual drug use, just one dose of ecstasy could have rendered her helpless and defenseless. That's the danger of ecstasy. It produced a mood changing euphoria, a phony feeling of well-being that, depending on the user's psychological and physical makeup and the specific combination of chemicals ingested could render them emotionally vulnerable, sexually aroused, and as unprotected as a guppy swimming with sharks.

As if that weren't bad enough, the ultimate effect of the toxic cocktail was unpredictable. Some kids only felt dizziness, nausea, and disorientation. The not so lucky died. Theo surmised that if Stella's toxicology report didn't list long-term cell damage in her brain tissues, it could only mean that she wasn't a heavy user. If not a user, then, it meant that something traumatic must have motivated her to take the drug, or worse, that someone had forced her to ingest a quantity large enough to cause the paralysis that stopped her heart.

Theo had never seen her friend under the influence. Stella was into running and healthy eating, not the usual pattern of behavior for someone into high stakes drug use.

"Would she willingly down that crap, or was she forced?" Theo murmured.

"What are you getting at, Theo?"

She didn't realize she had said loud enough for Jack to hear.

"I guess the report just poses more questions than answers for me, Jack."

"Me too. I want to know who she was with when she took that crap and why the son of a bitch didn't get her to a hospital!" He spat the words with all the pain and anger evident in his face.

"I don't know, Jack. But I intend to find out."

She glanced toward her desk and saw Stella's Journal. Theo stifled her sudden intake of breath. At that moment, Jack walked into the kitchen to help himself to more coffee. Theo walked over to the copy of the *Sun* spread on the couch, picked it up, and tossed it on top of the journal just as Jack looked up. She continued to tidy up.

"I do the same thing," he said. "I putter at anything to take my mind off it."

Theo leaned over against the counter with her mug extended. Jack poured the last of the coffee.

"You feel it too," she said, "It's as if Stella's guiding us somehow."

Jack leaned closer to her, and his eyes had a brightness that might have been hope.

"That's exactly how I feel. Like she's still here, pointing me onward toward something. I don't know what, but something!"

He put his head in his hands. His shoulders shook slightly. Theo knew he was crying. Theo gave him a few moments and moved into the sitting area. Presently, he wiped his eyes on his sleeve and stepped toward the window, staring across the patio at unit 2.

"Is that hers?" He asked.

Theo nodded.

"She loved flowers," Jack said.

"This is just the kind of place I'd have pictured her in." He said quietly.

"You need some rest," Theo said gently.

"Do you have a room?"

"Not yet," he said wearily.

"You could stay in Stella's cottage, if you like."

"Thank you, Theo. I'd like that."

Then, "Look, Theo, I've been thinking that I should talk to the police about Stella. See if they have any leads on what happened. What do you think about the police?"

She thought about Frank Marino snooping around Stella's unit and wondered if going to the police might connect Jack with Frank. She wasn't sure what that might mean, it just threw another complication into the equation. Her stomach tightened.

The only thing Theo knew for certain was that she needed time to piece together this puzzle. That was a luxury she didn't have. She needed to talk to someone about Stella's journal. She just wasn't sure if that person was Jack, at least not yet.

"So, what do you think?" Jack was asking her.

"About the police? That's certainly an option. Maybe it's something you'll want to do." She was buying time.

"Let's get you settled first."

Theo went to her desk and found the key. She grabbed linen and towels from her cupboard. Then, together, they walked the short distance to unit 2.

CHAPTER 38

As the door swung open, Theo held her breath thinking that Frank may have scattered Stella's personal items about.

The room appeared to be just as she had left it earlier that day. Nothing was out of place. The boxes hadn't been opened.

She stepped into the bathroom with the towels. That's when she noticed the bathroom window was unlocked.

That's how he got in! She thought. *He must have unlocked it when we were here earlier.*

The telltale trace of powered grout on the counter was the only other evidence of Frank's intrusion. She felt her stomach tighten. *He's figured it out. Now he knows that whatever was in that space is probably in my possession.*

"What time do you get started usually," asked Jack from the bedroom.

"Early," she said. "I write for a local paper."

She predicted an early-morning phone call from Sam as soon as he saw Oren's restaurant review and figured she'd be arguing with him for a while about it.

Theo brushed the powder residue into the sink and ran the water.

"My deadline's 10:00 a.m. So I'm on a tight schedule."

She hoped setting a timeframe should buy some time.

She walked over to the window, closed and locked it.

"Good. I'm hoping just to grab a few quick winks," Jack said.

"Could I get a cup of coffee from you later, then?"

"Of course," said Theo. "Just come over."

"OK, 'til then," he said and managed a weak smile. "And, Theo, thank you."

Theo smiled back. "Jack, I'm glad you're here."

CHAPTER 39

With Jack settled into Stella's unit, Theo started again on the journal. She read and reread the last entries but her eyes felt like sandpaper. A quick trip to the sink and a splash of cold water felt better. She poured a cup of cold coffee and nuked it in the microwave. KC was at the door.

"Get in here!" She admonished him.

"It's still dark! You'll be food for the canyon coyotes!"

The cat ignored her reprimand and leapt onto the desk. She saw it happen just at the crucial second but not fast enough to stop it.

KC stepped on the corner of the journal that protruded over the edge of the desk. It didn't hold his weight and both cat and journal crashed to the floor.

KC was only momentarily surprised at the mishap. He righted himself, gave a feline shrug or sorts, and then sauntered toward his food bowl as if nothing had happened.

Theo stared at the journal in a heap on her floor. She was riveted by something that stuck out from under the suede outer cover and the journal's inside flysheet. There were two loose corners of something that protruded – only they weren't Stella's handwritten pages – they were photographs.

The first was a picture of Stella with a man who she thought might be Ted Delaney. They were in a booth in a restaurant, both holding wine glasses in an apparent toast. They looked happy. With them at their table was a short swarthy-complexioned man, but he was no one Theo recognized.

The other photo was of a large yacht. It appeared to be moored at one of the boat harbors in San Diego. Theo thought the building to the right looked like the Sheraton Hotel or possibly the Marriott. She could barely make out the name on the stern of the boat. It looked like *Pair-A* something or other. There was more to the name, but it was obscured.

Theo was excited. She opened her Internet browser, accessed the newspaper archives and typed in *Ted Delaney*. Several backdated articles appeared. She clicked on the most recent, "City Councilman Ted Delaney Killed in Freeway Mishap." The photo was of Delaney's Mercedes wrapped around a tree on State Highway 163. Beside the accident photo was a file portrait shot of Delaney. There was no mistaking it – he was the man in Stella's photo.

So the mystery man in the first photo is Delaney, but who's the second guy? She thought.

Next, she accessed the City of San Diego's homepage and looked at the photos of the council members. No match.

She got up from the computer and started pacing. She worked the information over and over. Then, on a hunch, she returned to the city's webpage. Under the agendas for council meetings, she scanned several months worth and saw that action on zoning laws were listed three months in a row, but with no other cryptic information.

That's the beauty of public law requirements and the Brown Act, Theo mused, *government entities are required to make their agendas public, but they are allowed to list their impending actions by codified classifications. The obscure descriptions don't tell the average citizen what action might really be afoot. Unless you were on an inside track, there was much that could still be hidden.*

Frustrated, she closed the site. Her coffee had gotten cold again. She switched to tea. Holding the steaming hot cup, she breathed in the vapors.

She opened another website, the *Sun's* online newspaper; there, she typed "city council zoning laws" into the search window and waited.

Several listings appeared, but the one that caught her attention was "City Council to Consider Strip Club Zoning."

CHAPTER 40

Theo scanned the article written several months before. It reported an upcoming city council meeting to consider toughening restrictions on strip clubs in the Kearny Mesa and Midway areas.

The proposal was to strengthen existing zoning laws by requiring more distance between strip clubs and schools, churches, and other clubs, and it would require the police to vigorously enforce the no-touch ban between customers and entertainers.

Theo accessed the posted minutes of the council meeting. Embedded in the minutes, after public comment, were the remarks of council members. Among the comments was a statement that strong zoning laws were already in affect and that no action was needed to increase them. Then the council member stated that he thought it a waste of taxpayer money for police officers to have to spend time in the clubs to ensure that dancers and patrons maintained certain prescribed distances. He said that the officers' time would be better spent patrolling the streets to protect all the citizens. The speaker's name was Councilman Ted Delaney.

Then, in an interesting segue; Delaney suggested that the Council's Public Safety Committee review the no-touch restrictions with the police department. Delaney was chair of that committee.

Hmmm. Theo leaned back in her chair. *The no-touch rule kept nude dancers at least six feet from their customers and banned touching. If the committee was convinced by Delaney's claim, they could recommend repealing, or weakening the no-touch laws, knowing that the council would most likely rubber stamp that recommendation.*

Theo knew it was a stretch. And while it might be plausible, there really wasn't any proof to verify her theory.

Again, she accessed the city's Web page. She found the link for the Public Safety Committee and clicked on it. The names of committee members were listed: Ted Delaney, Chuck Feldspar, Lori Fischer, Bradford Thomas, and Mario Sanchez.

According to the donor sheets, Delaney, Feldspar, and Thomas had received $25,000 each, and all from the same donors.

Theo switched back to the *Sun's* archives. She scanned several articles related to city council matters without much luck. She was just about to give up when she clicked on the link to a brief item in the *Social Section.* It chronicled a fundraiser for a local charity for abused children and Councilman Delaney was mentioned as one of the speakers. The event was just a few days before his death.

She quickly reviewed the article – standard formula event reporting – what city dignitaries and high roller donors were there, what they wore, and the menu. Then a simple line from Delaney's speech caught her eye.

"And, ladies and gentlemen, we need to do all we can to protect this community's children from abuse. That means more police on the streets and available to respond to those critical calls. Law enforcement now wastes time and tax payer money patrolling bars and clubs enforcing archaic laws. We need those valuable public servants on the streets to protect its citizens and our kids!"

"Hmmmm, she mused, *Delaney was clearly on the side of the strip clubs, as least at this time he was.*

Theo clicked on the last link. It was a story on an earlier city council meeting that nearly turned into a riot. Strip club dancers and supporters faced off against a strong contingent of citizens who opposed such establishments. The two factions appeared to be engaged in a holy war of sorts in the middle of the council chambers.

The issue was whether or not the city council would approve a permit allowing yet another adult entertainment club in the Midway area. Community members claimed that one more club in that area would be an over saturation in the Midway commercial district for that type of industry. On the opposing side were those who claimed to be bartenders, dancers, and others who would be employed in the new club.

The dancers claimed First Amendment rights protecting artistic expression as their defense. Their opposition, ranging from parents to ministers, based their defense on alleged violations of decency standards. One particularly persuasive speaker, a local minister, described a dancer's performance. He was effusive in his account: "With her back to the customer, she repeatedly bent over in front of him, exposing her buttocks, then turning around and grabbing her clothed breasts with both hands, moving them in a circular motion, just inches from the man."

Theo cocked an eyebrow, smiling slightly. *And just how could he have known that? Does that come under the heading of ministerial oversight?* She chuckled to herself and continued reading.

The photos embedded in the article showed angry people carrying signs that read, "No More Strip Clubs" and "Save our Children."

On the opposing side, several pretty young women held signs that touted "First Amendment Rights." The photo of a man flanked by two pretty girls caught her attention. It was the mystery man in Stella's photo. The caption under the picture in the *Sun* article identified the man as the owner of a local club called the *Lion's Lair.* His name was Bobby Galpino.

CHAPTER 41

Theo typed *Bobby Galpino* into her computer's search engine. Several listings appeared.

She scanned down the list. Sandwiched between the listing for "Galpino's Restaurant in Cincinnati, Ohio," and the "Roberto 'Bobby' Galpino Fan Club" for an operatic singer, she found "M. Galpino Enterprises, Las Vegas, Nevada."

She clicked on that listing and stared at the screen. Luigi Maestro Galpino was the owner-operator of Stairway to Heaven: A "Gentlemen's Only" Club located on Las Vegas Boulevard, and the Pair-A-Dice all-nude adult review and casino on Riviera off the Strip. The last listing was a club in San Diego – the *Lion's Lair*. Its co-owner/operator was Bobby Galpino.

*   *   *

Theo leaned back in her chair and stared at the screen. It was falling together. She played it out in her head.

If Bobby Galpino wanted to guarantee a council vote that would protect his strip-club interests, he needed five votes. If the Public Safety Committee made the right recommendation, and if there was enough public support, most likely the item would get the council's nod.

Theo riffled through the mess of papers on her desk and found the wadded-up papers that were in Stella's envelope. They listed the councilmembers by name with dollar amounts. She did a quick calculation. Each of them received $25,000. She stared at the names, then she cross-checked them. The same donors, including Connie Tominsky, appeared on both lists.

Theo played it out in her head.

According to Stella's notes, Delaney was in on the deal. The donor lists showed that three council members, including Delaney, were paid $25,000, all from the same sources. One of those sources was Connie Tominsky, using money from Angel Martinez. But Connie wrote only one check to Feldspar's campaign. She never mentioned donating to Delaney or any of the others.

That means the donors' names are fronts. Someone funnels bribe money to three councilmen who are in powerful committee seats; the committee makes a recommendation to change the zoning laws or repeal the no-touch law and – voila! – those laws are off the books! Galpino gets a boost in his business interest. And each of the councilmen gets $25,000 or more added to their war chests.

"It's money laundering – and it's damn clever." Theo said out loud.

KC, who had been eyeing her through slanted slits, opened his eyes only slightly wider; he twitched an ear.

"That's right, KC," Theo said scratching the cat behind his ears, evoking a steady purring drone.

"It's not exactly a tape recording of the parties soliciting bribes, but it's very nearly a smoking gun!"

"And," she cooed to the cat, "who might care about such a scheme?"

KC had rolled over on his back, offering his rounded furry belly; she obliged and continued her monologue.

"This is how it works. The Feds limit political contributions from a single donor. Filter your money through many people – you get around it. Now! *If* you could prove that someone was using the strip club girls to funnel conduit contributions, you've got a clear violation of RICO."

So caught up in her soliloquy, Theo had momentarily stopped scratching KC's stomach. He opened an eye and willed her to continue. She did.

"*RICO* is the acronym for *Racketeer Influenced and Corrupt Organizations Act.*" Theo explained to the cat.

"Its how the Feds crack down on organized crime. Being investigated for a violation of RICO could be the kiss of death for an elected official's career. Being found guilty could put him and anybody else involved with him behind bars."

Theo smiled broadly.

"And that, my furry friend, is what's at the heart of this! These are high stakes for Bobby Galpino. The question is, were the stakes high enough for him to kill Delaney and," she paused, "Did he also kill Stella?"

Theo froze. She realized that Stella never actually said that Galpino was involved in the plot. *Maybe the lists aren't enough. Maybe there's more.*

CHAPTER 42

Theo went back to the journal.

Day 60: Switching gears! Back on track! What a merry-go-round weekend with Bobby! His yacht is gorgeous – what a party guy! Fun . . . exciting . . . laughs . . . no pressures . . . no commitment. With him, I'm me . . . the ME that's real . . . well, the ME I know. Why would I try to be any different??? No one knows what its like to live in my skin. Even Theo and Abby have no idea what its like to be me. I wouldn't want them to know – ever.

Bobby loved watching those corny pornos Juggie and I made. After, he played like we were filming him and me. He really liked that – it was fun! I felt free. Maybe when this is all over . . . maybe Bobby and I could spend some time together. He's fun and likes me even knowing what I am. I don't have to hide anything from him.

TD's left a dozen messages. I haven't returned the calls. *I can't. I can't see him . . . what could I possibly say?*

Day 70: Juggie says TD's on board. He congratulated me like I brought him in. The lamb to the slaughter . . . he said I "must be good."

Like I even know what "good" is. If TD's in, then maybe I won't have to see him again . . . I hope I never see him – ever!

I should be on cloud nine for what the payoff will be . . . instead I feel sick . . . sick. I've got an open-end ticket on United; I could just pack a bag, be gone out of this mess. I could just leave . . . I should.

Day 70 (night): *I spent four hours at the airport watching the marquee listing arriving and departing flights. All I had to do was pick one and get in line. I couldn't do it. I don't even know how many times I got in queue, and each time I'd get to the window and just change my mind. I think airport security assigned someone to watch me because I seemed so suspicious and odd. Finally, I left. I'm home now . . . my little house that I so love. I had a message from Juggie and five more from TD.*

I called Juggie. He seemed relieved to hear from me – wonder if he suspected I got cold feet? He told me to connect with TD and quick. I've never heard anything close to panic in Juggie's voice before tonight. I argued, said I didn't want to call TD. Finally, he convinced me. Time to tie up the loose ends . . . time to move on.

Day 71. *Town and Country Hotel in the Valley – I'll never forget it! I met TD there. He had a room. He wanted me. I did what I know how to do. I thought I could just be mechanical about it. I thought I could go through the motions – just seal the bargain. It doesn't work that way – not anymore – not for me.*

He made love to me, and I wanted it! After, he ordered room service . . . coffee and dessert . . . no booze . . . He said he wanted me to know that what he had to say was real – not the result of the liquor talking.

He held me and whispered it in my ear and held my face between his hands and said it again . . . and again. "I love you! I love you!"

I thought my heart would burst!

I told him it was crazy. He was married, and in politics!

He said his wife wanted a divorce anyway for different reasons and that she didn't even know about me. He said the job didn't matter, that he was resigning! He said we'd leave town; he was an attorney and could work anywhere. He said we'd be together . . . that he wanted to MARRY ME!

He said it was the right thing to do . . . He said it was what he wanted to do!

I don't think my feet touched ground! I started to cry and laugh . . . and I said, "OK!" Just like that . . . "OK!"

Day 72: *Reality hit me! TD doesn't even know me . . . the real me. He doesn't know my past . . . he doesn't know what I was paid to do and that I was part of the deal he's in with Juggie. He doesn't get it – not any of it – not yet.*

When he does, everything will change . . . only . . .

Stella didn't finish her thought; Theo felt her stomach tighten. She knew this was where everything fell apart.

> **Day 73**: *Today I told him . . . everything . . . all the ugly details.*
>
> *It was how he looked – like I kicked him in the stomach – he couldn't believe that I was part of the payoff. He was silent, but I could see his face turn like granite! Then he said, "When were you going to tell me, Stella, after you got your cut?"*
>
> *Just like that. Hard-edged and angry. I saw his love turn . . . to hate. No yelling . . . no punching . . . nothing. It was just over.*
>
> **Night**. *I'm sick . . . I hurt so bad inside . . . nothing can stop this pain . . . I'd take drugs if I thought it would work . . . but I know they don't. I'm a fool . . . a stupid, stupid fool . . .*

Theo's eyes were burning again, and the knot in her stomach tightened.

> **Another Day**. *I thought I'd feel less hurt now, but its worse. How can something so wonderful become so awful!*

> **Add Juggie**: *He's furious. Says TD's backing out, won't take the money – he's even threatened to go to the cops.*
>
> *I tried to call him, to plead, bargain, anything . . . He won't talk to me! He won't even listen to me! They'll ruin him. I begged him to see me to let me tell him how big this is and that he can't – they won't – let him back out now. He won't return my calls.*
>
> **Later**. *Finally! Juggie says he talked to TD, will meet him later for drinks at Dakota's. Says TD sounded like he wanted to see reason. If anyone can convince TD, it would be Juggie. I want this to work – it has to work for his sake. If I even knew how to pray, I would. Do you think there's anyone on God's payroll that hears people like me?*

The last entry was scribbled; the ink smudged.

> **Another Day**. *TD is dead. I want to cut out my heart to stop the pain! It was an accident – that's what they're calling it. They're blaming drugs and alcohol. He fell asleep at the wheel.*
>
> **I don't believe it**! *Open and shut . . . just like that! Only, TD didn't do drugs. That's the truth.*
>
> *Juggie said he never saw TD that night – he never showed. But he did see someone – the cop that's on Angel's payroll. Maybe he trusted the cop. "Maybe" is a big word but if he did, then it's all my fault. I pushed him. I drove him to it.*

I'm going to get Juggie to set me up to meet the cop. I'll know when I talk to him. I'll know then what really happened to TD. I've got to do the right thing for once . . . I'm overdue!

Theo couldn't believe the next part. It was directed to her.

Theo, you're reading this because I'm dead. I've sent this to you because you are in danger too. By now, you know I was involved in a scheme, but you don't know all of it. Take the papers with the lists of names to someone – **NOT THE COPS.** *Maybe the FBI –* I'm not sure . . . **DON'T TRUST THE COPS** *– your friend Marino is involved somehow. If he didn't kill TD, then he knows who did.* **BE CAREFUL!**

The hair on her neck stood up, and Theo went rigid as ice. For once, she couldn't reason herself away from what was staring her in the face.

Not Frank! How could it be? She couldn't believe that Frank was involved, yet she could still see his face in the pale light as he snuck out of Stella's unit just a few hours before. Theo couldn't ignore the mounting pile of evidence. The worst was Stella's warning and the nagging thought that he had something to do with Stella's death.

Theo thought about the FBI. She grabbed the phone book, found the listing and address. The offices opened at 7:30 a.m. She'd be there when they opened up for the day. For now, suddenly, she felt drained and exhausted.

Theo set her alarm for 7:00 a.m. She leaned back on the sofa and closed her eyes. In an instant she was asleep.

CHAPTER 43

O n some level of awareness, Theo knew she was dreaming. It was
the semiconscious kind that envelops you in a sensuous cocoon
and lulls you into thinking that you can control it.

She saw herself reclining on a blanket near the lakeshore. Why she was
at a lakeshore as opposed to any one of San Diego's gorgeous beaches wasn't
an important point to examine, so she simply accepted it, placing herself at
Lake Cuyamaca in the county's eastern mountains.

Her head rested in Frank's lap, and his fingers laced in and out of her
hair, caressing her face, slipping down her neck, gently toying with the open
button on her filmy lace top.

In the distance, someone was calling to them, but they were lovingly
focused on each other, absorbed with the smell and touch of skin, and the
stirring of excitement. They were drawing closer and consumed with the
intimacy of the moment.

He bent close and brushed her lips with his, moving over her cheek,
nuzzling her ear, then her neck. She turned her head slightly, yielding to his
touch. Each stroke connecting, electrifying every nerve, heightening senses,
drawing her even nearer to him.

But the woman's voice in the background grew louder and sounded like
Stella. Theo knew she had to open her eyes but didn't want to. She didn't
want to see Stella or know what it was she was trying to tell her.

She slipped her arms around his neck, pulling him down, closer, until
he was pressing against her. But suddenly, he turned away, looking toward
the voice, and he was forcing her to look out toward the middle of the lake
where Stella was swimming.

A strong sense of alarm washed over her, and the warmth of moments before evaporated, leaving a dry catch of panic in her throat.

Something was wrong. Stella was in trouble. Theo knew that Stella was drowning.

Suddenly, the man jumped to his feet and pulled Theo up with him. It was then that she saw that her lover wasn't Frank – it had been Jack. She struggled to free herself from him, but he was pulling her toward the water's edge. She knew he was going to pull her into the water. She pulled back as hard as she could, but she had no strength to fight his powerful grip on her wrists. She tried to shout, but her voice couldn't carry over the noise of someone pounding on the door. That's when she awoke.

Theo stared at the door, trying to focus her thoughts. The knocking continued. She stumbled to the door and opened it. Jack stood there with his empty coffee cup. He was smiling apologetically.

"Looks like I woke you. I'm sorry," he said, "I saw your light and thought you were up. Go back to sleep, Theo, I'll see you later."

At that instant, she wanted to tell him everything, rid herself of the pain and the anguish of everything.

"Jack?" He was halfway down the steps.

"Theo, you OK?"

She thought for a split second.

"Yeah, yeah, I'm fine. Just a little groggy, you know, working late, fell asleep. Please, come in, Jack. I think we both need something as strong and black as tar!"

CHAPTER 44

Theo made fresh coffee and handed Jack a mug. Still shaken by the feelings evoked by her disturbing dream and feeling a bit guilty, she avoided eye contact.

"Did you rest at all, Jack?"

"A little."

He was staring into his mug. He didn't seem to want to make eye contact either.

A loud thud on the screen door startled them both. Jack bolted to the door before Theo just in time to see the paperboy make the circular swing through the courtyard, tossing the morning news on the stoops of the other units.

Jack opened the door and retrieved the paper. He handed the morning edition of the *Sun* to Theo, and then settled back into the couch.

"You write for that one?" He asked.

"Used to."

"What happened?"

"It's a long story, Jack. I came up on the wrong side of the so-called religious right political machine trying to take over politics in what was my old beat. They decided I was 'Satan-incarnate' and turned up the heat, so to speak. I eventually just quit."

"Oh," He said, nodding in silent agreement.

"Those religious zealots can be brutal to sinners."

"Funny thing about people who hide their political agenda behind the Bible," Theo said. "To them, it's a form of religious war, so it justifies any behavior."

"Yeah," Jack said, "fanatics of any persuasion are dangerous."

"I decided a long time ago," Theo said quietly, "that just because you go to church, it doesn't necessarily make you a Christian anymore than standing in your garage makes you a car."

Jack shot her a sideways glance and smiled.

He finished his coffee, rinsed the mug, and set it on the sink.

"What's on the agenda for today?" She asked.

"I've got some business here in town. Later, I need to make funeral arrangements."

Theo stared at him feeling like all she'd done was try to find out who Stella really was and what she'd been involved in. She'd completely forgotten about the reality of dealing with her funeral and burial.

"Right." Theo muttered.

"Yeah," Jack said. "Would you mind coming with me to the funeral parlor a little later?"

Theo glanced at her clock. It was 6:30 a.m.

"I have a quick errand to run this morning. I should be back by noon."

"OK. I should be back then too. I'll just wait for you," he said.

CHAPTER 45

Jarvis Barkley glanced at his Rolex. He wasn't nervous, just eager. He had a great deal to be excited about. The escrow was closing on his, or rather Tommy Silver's property, and he was meeting the architect at 9:00 a.m. to view the model of his proposed new hotel complex downtown.

Everything had gone as planned with just a few minor hiccups. Jarvis had allowed for a few problems. That had been part of his plan when he convinced the city council members he bought that he was ready, willing, and financially able to build a money-making redevelopment project on San Diego's waterfront to benefit the city and bring wealth to its coffers.

The council was easily convinced, if not by his rhetoric, by the thousands of dollars he pumped into their private bank accounts. As a result, he was guaranteed the votes he needed to condemn fifteen blocks of prime real estate under the guise of redevelopment. It was an area that some saw as an eyesore community of shabby apartments populated by mostly low-income Latino families.

Barkley had eyed the property for sometime and was able to jump to action after a Supreme Court ruling that allowed local governments to seize private property, including people's homes, by the principle of eminent domain.

The doctrine of eminent domain had been on the books for decades. It wasn't anything new. In theory, it allowed local governments to acquire property for traditionally defined purposes such as building roads, etc. But the new ruling changed the face of the law. It allowed bureaucracies to use the rule to benefit a privately owned development project.

Barkley was elated. *It's a gold-plated bingo for me!* Barkley had cooed when he got the word from his Washington mole weeks before the ruling became public. The only other hurdle was approval by the Coastal Commission. Barkley's connections with a majority of the commissioners had already guaranteed a quorum in his favor.

The key to my success, Jarvis thought, *is making sure that problems are anticipated and evaporate before they can become disasters. And I am a master at eliminating problems.*

Jarvis walked over to the couch where Tommy Silver dozed and shook him.

"Man, no, *man,* come on, just a little more sleep." Tommy grumbled.

"*Tommy,*" Jarvis said softly, "Tom, my boy, we've got to get going. Lots'a work to do this morning, then you can sleep as long as you like and have everything you always wanted."

Tommy cracked bleary, swollen eyes, and tried to focus on Jarvis.

"OK, *OK.* Man, I need a drink."

"What you *need,* Tom, is a shower."

Jarvis helped him to his feet and got him into the shower, gingerly tossing Tommy's filthy, rumpled T-shirt and pants into the trash. He unzipped the clothing bag from *Nordstrom's* and laid out the Armani navy gabardine on the bed. Next, he unwrapped the white shirt and silk tie. Jarvis looked approvingly at the garments.

"Nice, if I say so myself! Today, Tommy my man," Jarvis said loud enough for Tommy to hear over the shower's spray, "you'll look like the prosperous businessman that you were destined to be. After those papers are signed, you'll be set and so will I. Hell, your whole family's gonna be set. So, scrubba-dub-dub!"

*   *   *

Jarvis parked in the underground parking garage and glanced at Tommy who looked perfectly calm, thanks to the shot of heroine Jarvis had administered just before leaving his downtown high rise.

"Now, remember, just sign the documents with your full name, eh, Tommy? Any questions, just look at me – I'll nod – you sign. Got it."

"*Yeah,* man," Tommy said softly, his eyes twinkling with the brightness brought on by the drug. "Man, this is *so* cool. And do I look sharp. Get me some great babes with this outfit." Tommy giggled.

"Great babes like money, Tommy. And soon, you'll be living the high life you've always wanted. I'll see to it."

Jarvis was thinking that taking care of Tommy might become a full time job, and like those bothersome blips in the road, he would have to take care of this one, permanently.

CHAPTER 46

Theo pulled into the parking lot of the FBI building in Kearny Mesa. The receptionist ushered her into a cubicle and told her to wait for Agent Willis. She didn't wait long.

"Ms. Hunter?" The trim tall black man said as he extended his hand and introduced himself.

He looked like a *GQ* ad. His expensive-looking suit and dark blue shirt hugged his muscular frame. The tie was a buttery Versace silk. Theo thought the image of the FBI had obviously changed for the better.

Agent Willis smiled at her and asked if she wanted coffee. She figured the charm was just to catch her off guard; she could tell he was sizing her up.

"No. Let's get to the point." Theo didn't want to waist any time.

"I have reason to believe that at least three and possibly five city councilmembers are involved in violations of the RICO statute. I have some information that creates a trail of conduit contributions to their election campaigns. The primary donor is the owner of several strip clubs in San Diego and Las Vegas. The illegal donations are bribes to influence the councilmen's votes."

Theo paused to take a breath. She eyed Willis for a reaction. There was none.

"I also believe that this club owner killed one of the councilmen and," she paused, "a dear friend of mine."

Now, Willis was staring at her hard.

"Who was killed and how did they die?"

"Councilman Ted Delaney and his girlfriend Stella Morris. Delaney was killed in a traffic accident. He was loaded on ecstasy and Quaaludes. Stella was found floating in the Tijuana Slough. She was also pumped full of ecstasy and other drugs. According to her autopsy, she was dead before her body was thrown in the water."

Agent Willis had pulled his computer keyboard toward him and was typing as fast she spoke.

"Just what would a strip club owner want from the councilmen?"

Theo continued. "The city council had recently considered stronger zoning laws that would have a negative impact on the strip clubs. A vote was coming up to increase the minimum distance between strip clubs and schools and residential neighborhoods."

"You have any documentation?"

"You can verify the council's action in their minutes. It's public information, you know."

"Thanks," Willis sounded annoyed. "I mean about the donations."

"I have a list of names of the donors here in San Diego and in Las Vegas." Theo said. "I don't have bank records, but that's something you guys have access to."

"Las Vegas donors to local councilmen's campaigns?" Willis raised an eyebrow. Theo nodded.

"Where's this list now?" He asked, not looking up from his keyboard.

"In a safe place," she said, eyeing him straight.

Agent Willis leaned back in his chair. His fingers suspended above the keyboard.

"If what you say is true, then, I doubt that any place you've hidden this information will be safe for very long." Agent Willis cautioned.

While she was telling her story, she had become flushed and excited. Agent Willis's admonition stopped her cold.

"You're saying I'm in danger?" Theo's bravado was more to calm her fears rather than an effort to bluff Agent Willis.

"How so? No one knows what documents I have."

Theo didn't reveal that Frank might suspect she had something, and she didn't mention his breaking and entering last night. Although she was close to blurting it out, she stopped short – she wasn't sure why exactly.

"You haven't shared this with anyone? Not even a girlfriend or boyfriend?"

Theo summoned what courage she had left and assumed a poker face.

"Look, Willis, I'm a reporter by trade and a damn good card player by design. I don't reveal my hand until I'm ready to cash it in."

Her words pumped up her nerve, plus, she was becoming irritated with what seemed like the typical condescending manner of men in law enforcement. Willis was beginning to remind her of Frank.

"Why didn't you go to the police?"

There it was – the question she dreaded. However she chose to answer, it would brand Frank Marino as a cop on the take and an accessory to murder. Again, for reasons more embedded in past loyalty than she could understand, she hedged.

"I thought RICO violations were under the purview of the Federal government," she said.

"Looks like you did your homework."

Agent Willis completed typing and hit the print key. While his printer worked, he leaned back in his chair and looked at Theo. She felt uneasy but didn't squirm. She stared back.

"If any of this is true, and I'm not saying it *is* since I don't have any proof other than your word to back up your claims, I don't think you realize just how much danger you might be in."

"OK, but some things – like putting the man or men who killed my friend behind bars – warrant a little risk, don't you agree?"

Willis didn't respond, but she thought the concept probably hit a chord. It was the kind of honor thing that men seemed to understand.

He continued, "I'm going to need whatever proof you have, the sooner the better."

"I'll get it to you later today – that soon enough?"

"How about I go with you to get it right now!"

It was a statement, not a question.

Theo thought about Jack waiting for her. It would be awkward if she showed up with Willis.

"Look, there's someone staying with me right now, and I don't want him to be suspicious about this."

"Who?" Willis asked.

"He's my friend, Stella's brother."

"The dead girl?" Again the eyebrow rose.

"Actually, Jack's staying in Stella's unit, which is across from mine. But he's waiting for me to come back. We have to make funeral arrangements. I'm afraid if you were with me he'd be suspicious."

"OK." Willis said. "But I need those documents ASAP today. I want to get on this thing before the leads get cold."

Theo stood to leave, but paused to ask a question.

"Will you have to notify the police?"

"Ms. Hunter, we're the FBI. We don't have to notify anyone."

She smiled dryly and turned to go, but Willis wasn't quite done yet.

"Who are you afraid of on the force?" he asked.

Theo didn't look back; she just shook her head.

"No one."

CHAPTER 47

Agent Willis watched her climb into her red Honda. She hadn't quite left the parking lot before he was on his cell phone.

The familiar voice answered on the first ring.

"Yeah," Frank Marino said.

"It's me. You were right. She's got some evidence, and its pretty damaging if it's all she says it is. She's going to bring it in later today. Sure. Damn right it's a problem. We don't want to fuck this up, and she's the one who can do it. You'd better handle it right this time!"

Willis snapped his cell phone shut and tossed it on the desk. He was getting nervous. There were too many involvements and too many loose ends. The last thing Agent Willis wanted was any chance that Theo's evidence would get into the wrong hands.

He picked up the phone and made another call. He wasn't going to let the whole thing blow up in his face.

* * *

Theo was on State Highway 163 and couldn't even remember leaving the building. She had protected Frank, and she still wasn't sure why. He was implicated in more ways than she cared to consider, yet she couldn't bring herself to accuse him publicly or privately. If the information Stella had was enough to incriminate Galpino, then, Frank's involvement, innocent or not, would surface on its own.

Deep down, she hoped that Frank wasn't tied to Stella's death. But after Stella's warning and Frank's break-in, his innocence seemed doubtful. No matter which way she turned it over, she couldn't continue to shield him from the FBI's scrutiny; that would surface on its own.

As she drove, she tallied the pluses and minuses involving Frank. The minus side far outweighed the plus. That's when she decided she couldn't buck those odds; she'd have to tell Willis about Frank this afternoon.

CHAPTER 48

When she pulled up in front of the cottages, she was still preoccupied with thoughts of Frank and didn't notice Jack watering Stella's flower baskets.

"Hey," he said, waving as she headed toward her unit.

Seeing Jack with the watering can brought Stella immediately to mind. She was instantly irritated with herself for dwelling on negative feelings involving Frank when she was sure he didn't deserve another concerned thought. Jack seemed to pick up on her mood instantly.

"You all right?" He asked.

"Oh, you know, Jack, some drivers are absolute assholes!"

"Sure," he said calmly. "I've met a few of those in my time."

"You waiting on me?" she asked.

"Yeah, I thought you wanted to go to the funeral parlor with me."

"Of course." She turned and started toward her car.

"Hey, I don't mind driving." He said. "I make it a habit not to drive with anyone who's as pissed off as you are."

Theo managed a weak smile, handed him her keys, and dutifully climbed into the passenger side.

* * *

Theo sat in the waiting room while Jack spoke with the funeral director. Although he had invited her in, she declined, feeling that this was a personal thing he needed to do for himself. She didn't want to intrude on something so intimate and private.

Comfort was emphasized everywhere in the luxuriously appointed waiting room. Soft pastel colors, brocade furnishings, and bouquets of fresh flowers.

It was the sweet floral scent that reminded Theo of her grandmother. It was one of the last smells she associated with her. Since her grandmother's funeral, Theo always connected the fragrance of cut flowers with mortuaries. Wherever she was, a wedding or some social event, the aroma took her back, bringing with it a sense of sadness.

Abby had told her that traumatic events heighten certain sensory perceptions and those perceptions can remain with you for years.

Forever touching the present with the recollection of the past, Theo thought.

"You OK?" Jack said softly.

So deep was she in thought that she hadn't heard him approach and was startled at his voice.

"Oh, yeah, yeah, I'm fine," she said. "I should be the one asking you, Jack."

"I'm alright," he said. "I've come to terms with this. Let's go."

*   *   *

Jack pulled up in front of the cottages and handed Theo her keys.

"Listen," he said. "I've got some business to take care of. If you don't have dinner plans this evening, I'd like you to be my guest."

"I'd like that," Theo said.

"Great! I like late dinners. How about 8 o'clock?

"That sounds fine, 8 o'clock it is," she said.

*   *   *

Theo dialed Agent Willis and got voice mail. She hung up not wanting to leave a message. She thought she'd try him again in an hour.

CHAPTER 49

It was payday for the employees of the Lion's Lair. Connie Tominsky pulled her Nissan Sentra into the employee's section of the lot. She would have been there sooner if her early morning class at the university hadn't dragged on.

Her biology professor – Connie labeled him "Dr. Drabble" – droned on forever, then finally issued the class assignment, which was to read and synopsize the recent EPA report about finding *E. coli* in recreational water samples and the risk of gastrointestinal illness associated with swimming in that water.

While the topic was fascinating and more than relevant to daily living, the research alone required more than the three hours a week after-class time that Connie had already allotted on her study schedule. Along with the hours, she spent on her full time job, Connie figured she'd be lucky to net four hours sleep the next two days. She was mentally rearranging her schedule when she eased into a slot marked "compact."

There were three other vehicles in the lot, but she recognized only two of them, Angel's Cadillac Escalade and the bookkeeper's Volvo. The third was a large black truck and belonged to no one she knew.

"I was beginning to think you didn't need the money." Doris the bookkeeper said as she handed over the check after Connie signed the payroll control sheet.

"Well, Doris, this baby's spent before I even get it!"

"Ain't that the truth." Laughed Doris. "Mine, too, honey. Always has been, probably always will be."

"You know," Doris said, "you could probably make a lot more if you started dancing. I can tell you, those girls do damn well."

"Yeah, it's not like I haven't thought about it, but I don't exactly relish being ogled by testosterone-challenged middle-aged drunks or those raging-hormone jarhead marines, if you know what I mean," answered Connie.

"Listen, honey," Doris said in a tone of motherly advice, "You just keep doing what you're doing, don't waste your money, and keep your little butt in college, and one of these days you can say *sayonara* to this joint."

"Say," Doris added, "wha'cha studying anyway?"

"Microbiology," Connie replied. To Doris's quizzical look, she explained, "It's the study of viruses and infectious diseases. Maybe someday I'll be a doctor that stops an epidemic."

"Well," Doris looked pleased, "that's terrific, honey, you keep at it."

"Thanks, I plan to."

As she started to leave, Connie remembered that she left a textbook in her locker. She headed back to the dressing room area and was just passing Angel's office when she overheard voices. Angel's tone made her stop. While she didn't ordinarily eavesdrop, he sounded agitated and a little frightened.

"I know," Angel stammered, "but I've only got so many folks here who can donate. Hell, I've even used my wife and my dead mother. Seems like the Vegas team needs to ante up. We're tapped out here."

"Angel, *Angel*," the male voice crooned," it's not like you have to ante up out of your own pocket. The money's a *gift*, you just need to come up with the names of donors. That's all we're asking. You're not putting in 110 percent on this, and I'm afraid that's been noticed by the big guys."

The stranger continued.

"Listen, I have to call Feldspar and tell him the money's in. He'll do his part, but we have to do ours. And we can't do ours if we don't have names. Got it?"

"Hell, yes," replied Angel, "I *got* it. I've used my employees and my whole family. Shit! It's not like I can call in the PTA and the church guild if you know what I mean!"

"I hate to say this to you, Angel, what with you trying to be so helpful and all, but you know, accidents *do* happen."

CHAPTER 50

A ngel started to cough. Connie heard the sound of liquid being poured into a glass. Then the stranger spoke.

"Hey, I'm your friend here. I'm not trying to threaten you, man. It's just that I have some heavies pushing on me. You know how that it is. I can't take a whiz what they're peering over my shoulder."

Angel laughed nervously.

"Yeah, I know, we have to pull together on this," Angel added.

The stranger's voice was soothing.

"Right. *Right*, man. Now, I've got Feldspar chomping at the bit for this dough. He's nervous as hell. Feldspar won't play if we don't move the money. We can't move the money if we don't get names. You know how these politicians are. They panic and do stupid things. Remember Delaney. I don't want to have any more accidents. But, you know, my boss won't take any chances. Get what I mean? That's just how it is. Shit! It just complicates the whole fuckin' deal – for all of us."

"*Jeezus*," Angel hissed, "are you fuckin' threatening him too? That guy'll pee his pants if you push him like that."

"Well," the other man said, "Galpino's getting antsy. He's had his hands in Uncle Louie's till too long, and he's sweating it. He can't afford to have anything touch his bottom line. He's got to get that item voted down. If those new ordinances go through, he'll have to close this place. That's when Uncle Louie finds out he's been cheating him. He can't take that chance. He's peeing blood right now he's so scared. You know Galpino, he doesn't handle 'scared' very well. I wouldn't want to be in his line of fire if this whole thing blows up."

"*Shit!* It's his own damn fault." Angel spat angrily.

"He's living high on the hog like a goddamn sultan, and he keeps bleedin' us. Pisses me off!"

Cigarette smoke drifted out the crack in the door, and Connie covered her nose. She needed to get out of there undetected before her allergies kicked in, and she started a sneezing fit.

She slipped past the doorway, but stopped when the stranger started to speak again.

"Look, we've been romancing this prick Feldspar long enough. I'm done with the *foreplay,* if you know what I mean. If this guy doesn't put out then we'll just have to find another way, probably one he won't like too much. Only thing, though, Angel, too many accidents raises suspicions. We really don't want that. So you come up with the names, I give the dough to Feldspar, he votes our ticket, and – *voila!* – everybody's happy!"

"Yeah," Angel said, "OK, *OK,* I get the picture."

He rubbed his chin nervously. The wheels were obviously turning. Then he brightened.

"*Hell!* People are dumb enough to sign petitions all the time in front of supermarkets. They give away their names and address and half the time they don't even know what it's for. I'll see if I can't get some of the girls out there with bogus petitions in front of *Von's* or *Ralph's.* We'll convince them it's to protect zoning."

The stranger sounded friendlier.

"*That's* the ticket, Angel. That's all I'm saying, just get me the names. I'll take care of Feldspar. He's ready to go with it, just wants his money up front. Like I said, he's a real dumb shit, *and* he's greedy. It's a perfect combination!"

Angel laughed.

"OK! It's done and *done!*"

"I knew you'd come through, Angel. Just don't screw up," the stranger said.

"I have more business than I need right now, and I don't like working overtime. Know what I mean?"

"Right, *right,*" said Angel, a little too fast.

"No problem. I'm on top of it."

Their voices were close to the door now. Connie darted into the restroom just as the office door swung open and Angel and his visitor headed down the hall. She held her breath as their voices receded. She waited what seemed like a very long time. She wanted to be sure they were long gone before she stepped out into the hallway. She forgot about her textbook. All she wanted was to get out of there before Angel or his visitor saw her and figured she might have overheard them. She was just rounding a corner approaching the front door when Angel saw her.

"Hey, Connie," Angel said surprised.

"What're you doing here?"

Shit! She thought. *Be cool or he'll suspect something's up.*

Connie waved at Angel and continued toward the door.

"Hi, Angel, just picked up my check and was talking to Doris," Connie managed to say brightly.

"Doris ain't here," he said.

"Oh, guess she left when I had to use the john. Well, see you tomorrow night. Take it easy, Angel."

Connie kept up her pace. She managed to get out the door and into her car, but not before Angel's visitor noted her car and license.

"Who's she?" he said in low clipped voice.

Angel caught the visitor's menacing tone. He tried to act nonchalant. "Her? Oh, just a waitress. She just stopped in to pick up her check."

"She might have overheard us." The visitor sounded wary.

"And that, my friend, is a problem."

"Naw," said Angel. "She don't know nothin'. She's just a dumb kid. She's nice too."

"*Jeezus*, Angel," said the visitor sarcastically.

"Your reasoning powers are phenomenal. You'd make a hell of a lawyer. What's *nice* got to do with snooping around? Just 'cause she's *nice* doesn't mean she's deaf. We were talking pretty loud, and you left your door open, remember? Galpino doesn't take any chances and neither do I."

"Aw, shit!" Angel whispered. "She's just a kid."

The visitor turned his cold hard stare on Angel. "Get me her address." He hissed. "*Do it!*"

CHAPTER 51

Connie's heart was racing, and she tried hard not to let the same emotion show in her driving as she barely managed to keep the car within the speed limit. What she overheard terrified her.

Theo had been right. She had been involved in a scheme to influence a politician, and it was more than just a little under-the-table money, much more.

Connie hadn't really worried about the money because she figured Angel knew what he was doing. Now, hearing how frightened he was left her feeling deserted, unprotected. If the mystery man could intimidate Angel and threaten a politician, then she could be in serious danger, especially if he thought she had overheard them.

Connie was so scared she felt sick.

She headed straight for Abby's place. She decided she'd tell Abby everything. Connie was banking on Abby's logical, problem-solving approach to help her distance herself from all this.

She decided there was no way she could ever set foot in the Lion's Lair again. But one thing was certain, she had to find another job without sending suspicious signals to Angel, and it had to happen immediately.

* * *

Abby didn't answer at home. Connie headed for Bailey's. As she figured, Abby was doing the books in her cramped little office cubicle. She looked up and smiled as Connie slipped into the chair.

"Hey," Abby said. "Nice surprise. What're you up to?"

Connie's started talking, words tumbling over each other. Then, she started to cry. Abby held her. Finally, when her sobbing subsided, Abby spoke slowly.

"Look, first of all, they don't know that you overhead them. Right?"

"Right," Connie answered thoughtfully, "I think."

"But you acted normal when you talked to Angel, so chances are he bought your story. All you need to do is not let him think you suspect anything."

Connie swallowed a sob and sniffled. She was listening.

"You have to go to work tomorrow night." Abby said matter-of-factly.

Connie's eyes widened in horror, and she started to shake her head no.

"Connie, you have to act like everything's OK. I know it's a bluff, but you can do this, you can!" Abby's tone was serious and encouraging, like a coach sending a player back onto the field after a nasty tumble.

"Then," she continued, "next week, tell Angel you're taking an extra class and have to cut back on your hours. He's not going to like that. So then you tell him you realize that might be putting him in a bind and you think it would be best if you just found another job that works with your class schedule. Offer him two week's notice. He'll tell you that he'd like to start someone else right away. You agree. Bingo! You're a winner, and Angel's no wiser." Abby reasoned.

"But I don't have another job. I need to work. I have bills and school and . . ." Her tears started again.

"Yes, I know." Abby cupped the girl's face in her hands and gently forced Connie to look at her.

"Listen, you need another job, and right now, I'm up to my ears in bookwork *and* bar work. I need someone to help me. You could do that. You know how to mix drinks, and you're good with customers. I can't pay you what you made there, but maybe you could cut expenses. You could move in with me for a while, just until you can find a something that pays more. Then, when you're back on your feet, if you want to, you can move out. No strings for either of us. How's that sound?"

Connie brightened. "You'd do that? Let me move in with you? Give me a job?"

"You're very special to me, Connie. I'm not saying that either one of us needs to make a commitment right now. It's just two friends helping each other out. But it's up to you."

Abby handed her a Kleenex. Connie blew her nose and nodded.

"OK," she said thickly.

"Listen, you go to your place and get some clothes. You need to stay with me tonight. OK?"

Connie sniffled and blew her nose once more. She hugged Abby and giggled a tiny nervous laugh. Then she started to cry all over again.

CHAPTER 52

H e answered his cell phone on the first ring.
"Yeah!"
"I've got a job for you," Jarvis Barkley said.
"You must love to pay overtime!" Juggernaut said.
Barkley ignored the sarcasm and got to the point.
"My sources tell me that Feldspar is getting nervous."
"That source wouldn't be Angel now would it?"
"Indirectly, yes," Barkley said. "He's concerned about some waitress that may have overheard you two this afternoon. He thinks you might be taking care of her. You know what I mean?"
"So what's the deal?" He was irritated.
"Angel's getting cold feet, doesn't like the complications of our type of business, which raises concerns for me about the whole strip club connection. It wouldn't be good for *my* business, if you get my drift." Barkley snapped.
"Your deal is getting very problematical. Solving problems costs more."
"You need to take care of that waitress," Barkley said.
"That was on my agenda."
"And Angel too," Barkley said.
"I thought you wanted Feldspar wrapped up. Angel's just trying to get the final names so we can cash him out. So taking care of Angel might not work in the long run."
"Like I said, its time to dump the whole city council-strip club connection. Taking care of Angel is in my plan."
"I'm listening," said Juggernaut.

"My sources tell me the FBI may be onto the city council payoff scheme. That's going to break soon. When the FBI gets in the act, the media will have a raw meat feast. They'll be so busy pointing fingers that my little land deal will go virtually unnoticed. Escrow's closing any day now. What I need most is not to have waitresses or nervous strip club managers talking – to anyone."

"So you never planned to help Galpino out of his little dilemma?"

Barkley laughed.

"Like I give a crap about Galpino! Besides, when his uncle finds out he's been skimming those clubs his ass will be grass and Uncle Louie the mower!"

Barkley laughed again at his own joke.

"I just needed to line up the city council. The strip club donations were a ruse. The parties, the girls, the money, it all worked to rook 'em in. Once they were in, getting them to vote my way on the land deal was no problem. They couldn't afford to displease me. I had the goods, and they knew it."

"You slick bastard!" Juggernaut laughed.

"I knew you'd appreciate my plan."

"So I just need to have you sew up these few little loose ends. *Capisce?*"

"By loose ends you mean Angel and the waitress?"

"You're quick!"

"Well, *that* kinda quick requires suitable compensation. Like I said, complications cost more."

"What's your price?" Barkley was guarded.

"I'm going to need $100,000 more."

"*Jeezus,*" Barkley yelped.

"You're already in for nearly a mil on my big deal. This is just part of it. If all goes as planned, you'll be rich. I see your job as salary, not piecemeal. You do what needs to be done. That means Angel and anybody else that's in the way. You see it any differently?"

"Well, I'm doing the dirty work and taking the chances. I get caught, and I'm the one doing time."

"You get caught and my whole deal implodes. That's a goddamn big risk for me, *too*, don'cha think?" Barkley voice went up two octaves.

"So if I get you right, originally, I was just supposed to line up the big diversion so your land deal could slide through without a hitch. I kept my end of the bargain. But my job keeps getting tougher, and I'm not getting a raise."

"You don't get it." Barkley was shaking now.

"I'm taking the risks. I'm the one in the social scene and in the papers. If my name gets linked to any of this my plans evaporate like so much dust!"

There was a pause on the other end of the phone. The response when it came was calm with a touch of menace.

"I want $100,000 extra for these two *extra* jobs. I'm not asking, Barkley, I'm telling you my price or the loose ends get left to dangle. And you, well, lets just say I don't like getting stiffed."

"OK, OK! *Goddamnit*! This is *not* how our deal should work! Barkley was angry and scared and every bit of it showed in his voice.

"Don't pee your pants over this," Juggernaut said calmly.

"I don't want to screw up this deal anymore than you do. From my perspective it's just risk management, nothing more than an extra rider on your insurance policy. A hundred grand is just the premium."

Barkley felt trapped.

"OK, *alright*, then. You'll take care of the two problems, and you'll get your premium!"

Barkley heard the line click. It would be a while before he calmed down. He tried to rationalize this next hiccup in his plan. He hadn't expected to be involved in four murders. But each part of the plan had to fit together for success. Any irregularity was an added risk.

He's right. I've got too much invested now to screw this deal. What's an extra hundred-grand? He'll sew up the loose ends and no one's the wiser. Safer is wiser.

Barkley's breathing slowed a little. He was beginning to calm down. He lit a cigarette, took a long drag, and exhaled steadily. *Yeah, I'm too close to let this unravel. I've tightened it up. No loose ends. It's my game of hardball now.*

CHAPTER 53

The dinner hour line at Filippi's Pizza Grotto in Little Italy snaked through the delicatessen at the front of the restaurant and out the door.

The smell of fresh garlic bread and the heady aroma of classical Italian dishes wafted through the deli whetting the appetite and driving gastronomical senses crazy.

In the best of times, the line moved quickly; at peak lunch or dinner hour, not so much. At its worst, you might have to linger by the wooden crates of salted dried codfish.

Those who waited outside at the queues tail end had a front row seat – so to speak – of the flurry of tourists and local characters that spilled out of the variety of eateries, bakeries, and other businesses that lined India Street in Little Italy.

"Sorry about the wait, Jack," Theo said apologetically, "but the *ambience* really starts at the door!"

Surprisingly, the line moved quickly, and soon Jack and Theo were seated at a cozy nook with requisite checkered tablecloth and shakers of grated cheese and dried red-pepper flakes under a canopy of straw basket-wrapped Chianti wine bottles that dotted the ceiling like a thatched-roof patch work.

The family-owned eatery was a popular local landmark and had been for fifty-plus years. The food was good and inexpensive, and the atmosphere family oriented. It was one of Theo's favorites.

Jack ordered a bottle of the Rufino Chianti and the antipasto salad for starters. The menu was a delightfully daunting dilemma, deciding entrées took a little longer. Finally, Jack settled on meat lasagna and Theo the eggplant parmigiana.

They kept the chatter light, sipped their wine, and devoured the food with exceptional gusto. Theo didn't broach the subject of Stella and Jack didn't either.

Italian coffee and crispy cannoli were dessert. Jack said he hadn't eaten that much since his first day home from the army. Theo complained that another bite of anything would result in a zipper malfunction. They both said how much fun it had been.

They were standing in front of Theo's place, talking for awhile when Connie drove up.

"Hi-ya!" Connie chirped as she sauntered up to them. Theo introduced Jack.

"I'm so sorry about Stella," Connie offered apologetically. "She was so sweet to me and Abby. We'll miss her. I know you will too."

"Thanks. Yeah, I will," Jack replied.

"Well, Theo, it was fun. It's late, and I don't think either one us has much sleep these last few days. Can I get coffee from you tomorrow?"

Theo smiled and nodded. "Anytime, Jack."

The moon sat low in the eastern sky. The slow assent of the silvery disk and the chill in the night air reminded Theo that fall was approaching.

Time marches on, she thought, *as must we all.*

CHAPTER 54

It was dark when Abby slipped on her hooded sweatshirt and slid behind the wheel of Connie's Sentra and set off for Fashion Valley Mall.

She didn't pay any attention to the large black truck that followed her as she wound through Hillcrest, turning on First Avenue past the Jack in the Box, and left onto Bachman Street, a little known back road that led from Hillcrest, curving down a steep descent to the floor of Mission Valley.

She had just looped past the UCSD Hospital parking structure and rounded the first curve. It's a brief stretch of road with no street lamps; the only illumination came from the pale moon and the Sentra's headlamps on the road winding ahead.

She never saw the truck until it tapped her rear bumper. Then, with a hard push, it locked onto it. She was being forced off the road and over the side of the berm and into the canyon and she was powerless to stop it.

The little car slid several feet down the incline, and then tore into the scrub brush with a sickening metallic crunch. The force of the impact shattered most of the front end and jammed the steering wheel hard into Abby's chest. The truck sped away as the little Sentra's horn howled in the otherwise still night.

CHAPTER 55

Finally, exasperated after several tries that afternoon without connecting with Willis, Theo left a message on his voice mail. She fell asleep waiting for his call.

It was the phone's ringing that woke her. She fumbled with the receiver and mumbled, "Hullo?"

"Theo Hunter?" The man's voice was all business.

She was immediately awake.

"Agent Willis, I've been trying to reach you."

"Are you Theo Hunter?" the man asked again.

"Who is this?" she demanded, suddenly uneasy.

This is Sergeant Johnson with the San Diego Police Department. Ms. Hunter, do you know Abby Archer?"

Theo felt her chest tighten. Her throat went dry, and she swallowed hard.

"Yes. Is something wrong?"

"You were listed as an emergency contact number. I'm sorry to report that there's been an accident."

"Please tell me she's OK." It was a plea not a question. Sergeant Johnson's tone softened.

"Your friend has been taken to Mercy Hospital. She's in critical condition. I don't know the extent of her injuries."

The news that Abby was alive was the spark that gave her hope.

"Where did it happen? On the freeway?"

"Actually, it was on Bachman Street. It looks like she lost control of the vehicle and plunged over the embankment down into the canyon. It's a miracle that the car's exhaust didn't ignite a brush fire. A bicyclist heard the horn and saw the lights. Your friend is lucky. If it hadn't been for him, she might have been there for hours before being discovered. There are no street lamps in that section of the road. She might not have been found until daylight."

Theo took in everything the officer was saying, but her mind was racing. She urgently wanted to get to the hospital. She wrapped up the information the officer needed and hung up.

Theo glanced at her clock, it was 12:30. She didn't have a number for Connie, so she dialed Abby's number. She didn't know if Connie was planning to stay with Abby that night or not, but she left a message for Connie on Abby's voice mail.

She grabbed her bag and darted out the door. Just as she was about to drive away, she thought about Jack. Thinking she might not return until morning, Theo thought she should leave him a note. She fished around in her bag, found her notepad, and scribbled a few lines about having an emergency at the hospital. She left her cell phone number and asked him to call her. She wedged it between the screen door and the jamb of unit 2.

CHAPTER 56

Angel Martinez reached his SUV just as the man stepped out of the shadows.

"Shit!" Angel said. "You scared the crap outta me! What's up?"

The man didn't respond; he simply pulled his weapon and fired. Twice.

Angel fell back against the SUV, stunned. Another muffled shot, and Angel felt his insides turn to ice.

Angel's eyes were still open when the man pulled his wallet from his bloody jacket pocket. The last thing Angel saw was the cold hard eyes and a smile that curled slightly at the edges of his killer's mouth.

CHAPTER 57

Theo gave her name as next of kin to the emergency ward nurse and was told that Abby Archer was in the ICU. The nurse wouldn't disclose anything else. Theo thought that was a bad sign.

She expected the worst when she was ushered into Abby's room; what she saw just confirmed her fears.

Abby was unconscious and hooked up to a breathing machine. Her head was bandaged, and there was a cast on her arm. There was a tent over her chest area.

Theo took the chair at the bedside.

Through most of the night, she watched the heart and breathing monitors until her eyes grew heavy and closed. She nodded off a couple of times, but forced herself to stay awake by remembering Abby and the antics of two girls, fast friends, who kept true to each other as if they were bonded by blood. She focused on the good times, and as memories have a way of doing, the vignettes offered glimpses of childhood from a distant all-knowing perspective. Finally, she couldn't fight it anymore and drifted off to sleep.

*   *   *

It was a little after 3:00 a.m. when Theo was awakened by a gentle shake. Connie's pixy face was pale, and she looked frightened. They hugged, and Theo found herself struggling to hold back tears while Connie sobbed quietly.

A young doctor came in and introduced himself. Theo said she and Connie were next of kin.

The doctor explained that, while Abby's injuries were significant, they had been downgraded to non-life-threatening. Abby had sustained broken ribs and a broken arm, as well as a bruised sternum and a concussion. He said the padding on the steering wheel had impacted her chest at just the right angle to protect her from fatal damage. He said she was lucky.

The doctor's news was more than just a relief; it lifted the burden of anguish, replacing it with hope. The two hugged again, and this time, Theo didn't hold back her tears.

CHAPTER 58

Theo and Connie stayed by Abby's bed side into the dawn. They took turns with catnaps until Abby awoke sometime around 7:00 a.m.

When she opened her eyes, they were having coffee and talking softly. She tried to talk, but both patted her free arm and told her to rest.

Theo explained quietly what had happened and told her that she would recover fully. Abby attempted a weak smile, then drifted back into unconsciousness.

It was nearing noon when Theo headed home. She remembered to try Agent Willis again. Rummaging through her bag for her cell phone, she suddenly remembered that in her rush to get to the hospital she had left her cell phone charging on the kitchen counter.

Brilliant, Theo, she chided herself. *You give Jack the number then leave the phone at home!*

She tried Agent Willis from a pay phone in the lobby and only got his voice mail again. This time, she left brief message about a family emergency and asked him to call her back to confirm a time for her to get the journal to him.

Driving home, she thought how close she came to nearly losing Abby and how devastating that prospect had been. Then, she thought about Jack and how he must feel having lost Stella.

I can't keep that journal from him any longer. I'll share it with him before I take it to Willis. It's only right. Jack deserves that. It's what Stella would want.

CHAPTER 59

J ack wasn't home when she arrived. Theo took a quick shower and slipped into a fresh top and jeans. She heard the truck's door slam and saw him heading toward Stella's unit.

"Jack!" she yelled through the screen door.

"Hey!" he called back.

"Found your note, but I had to go out last night. I tried your cell, but you didn't answer," he said, crossing the patio.

"I forgot it at home," Theo said apologetically.

"So how's your friend?" Jack was saying as he crossed the patio in her direction.

"Oh, Jack, something terrible has happened."

He spanned the short distance quickly and followed her inside. She closed the door behind him and stood there not sure where to begin. When she started to speak, her voice cracked. Hot tears started down her cheeks.

"My friend Abby was in a terrible accident last night. She's badly hurt."

"How? Where?" He said.

"She borrowed her friend Connie's car. She was on Bachman and somehow lost control. She went down an embankment. Oh, Jack, she was nearly killed!"

Theo was barely able to speak through her sobs.

Jack looked stunned. Then he reached out and put both hands on her shoulders and pulled her to him. He held her close, rubbing her back until the sobbing subsided.

"Is she going to recover?"

Theo was sobbing and couldn't quite answer. She nodded the affirmative against his chest.

"Then, it all be OK," Jack said quietly. "She's alive, Theo."

His words were calming. Presently, the sobbing subsided, and Theo became aware of the warmth and the closeness of him. At that moment, he very gently, tilted her chin upward and kissed her on the lips. It was as if the torrent of emotions welled up inside her had suddenly spilled out into a passionate urgency she couldn't control. She feverishly returned his kiss, clinging to him, yielding to every touch, lost in his compassion and hungry for his warmth.

After a few minutes, he gently eased away and settled her on the couch.

"Theo," he said softly, "we have to talk about a lot of things."

"I know, Jack. I have so much to tell you. I'm sorry I didn't tell you sooner, it's just that I . . . ."

"Tell me what, Theo?"

"I mean, I meant to all along, it's just that everything has gotten so out of control and I . . . ."

"Theo, *tell* me!"

"I found documents that Stella left, incriminating documents that might lead us to her killer."

This was the first time that Theo had verbalized the obvious and the word *killer* hung in the air between them. Jack's eyes narrowed, and he looked hard and angry.

"What kind of documents?" he asked.

"Her journal," Theo said, "with the names of people who donated to election campaigns for city councilmen. There's reference to a local strip club owner with a Las Vegas connection. I've researched it, and I believe those donations skirted campaign reporting laws to buy city council votes."

"Stella wasn't very political, Theo. Why would she be involved in something like this?" He said thoughtfully.

"Jack, I don't want this to shock you, but do you really know what Stella did for a living?"

She watched him carefully for his reaction, but there was none. She continued.

"Her journal talks about entertaining for money. Do you know what I mean?"

"You need to be more specific." Jack's tone had a hard edge to it.

"She entertained men for money, Jack. One of those men was Ted Delaney, *Councilman* Delaney. Her journal says she was working with a partner, someone named Juggie and that he was the connection with the money for the strip club interests."

"Jack, I think this Juggie killed Stella."

"What else does the journal say?" He said softly.

"Mostly about how she loved Delaney. His death was the turning point for her. Jack, she tried to get out of this mess, and I'm certain that Juggie is responsible for Delaney's death, too."

"Does she say who Juggie is? Jack asked quietly.

"No. She doesn't. But I think he's someone she's known for some time. She mentioned some history with him and . . ." Theo stopped, not sure she could say the rest.

"And . . . what?" Jack's voice rose sharply.

"And she mentioned something about films. She may have been involved in pornographic films, somehow."

Theo stopped; she felt she'd said far too much. She couldn't read Jack's reaction to all this. He looked angry or hurt. He stood and walked toward the kitchen.

"I don't know about you but I need a drink."

He poured scotch into two glasses and brought one to Theo. Jack downed his in one gulp. Theo sipped it, and then finished the glass.

"Want another?" He asked.

Theo closed her eyes and felt the fiery liquid slide down her throat. This time there was no coughing and the effect was quickly calming.

She didn't open her eyes for what seemed a long time, she didn't want to see the disappointment and hurt in his face. When she did, he was standing over her, a soft smile played at the corner of his mouth. Then he sat beside her and started to massage her shoulders again. The scotch was taking effect rapidly, and she was beginning to feel warm and strangely limp.

"Who else knows about the journal? Where is it now?" He asked softly.

"I met with the FBI yesterday, but I didn't give it to him."

"You still have it, Theo?"

"Uh-huh," she said.

His hands moved slowly down her shoulders across her breast and back up. The sensation was dreamy and electric at the same time. She was smiling when he placed his lips on hers and pushed his tongue deep into her mouth.

Theo opened her eyes, but all she saw was a soft glow all around Jack's head. His hands were deep inside her shirt, caressing her nipples. She tried to raise her head, but it felt like lead. He was whispering in her ear.

"Theo, where is it?" he asked, again.

At that moment, she would have told him anything he wanted to know, but the distance between the desire to respond and her audible voice seemed impossible to bridge and his words were slipping so far away.

Theo drifted there in the fuzzy, glowing place for what seemed like forever, then she slid into unconsciousness.

CHAPTER 60

The insistent buzzing of his cell phone as it vibrated on the nightstand bore into his sleep. It took a couple of seconds before Frank Marino realized what it was.

"Yeah," he mumbled, flipping the lid and growling into the transmitter. "This had better be good to get me outta bed!"

"We've got a problem!" snapped Bobby Galpino. "Angel's dead and it ain't no robbery like the cops claim."

Frank was sharply awake now.

"When? How?"

"Sometime this morning, after he closed the club. Three shots, point blank. They took his wallet to make it look like a robbery. Angel's keys to his Caddy were in his hand. Any robber would'a taken 'em. This ain't no goddamn robbery!"

Bobby continued, "Angel called me last night to say the Juggernaut was out of control. He admitted to Angel that he'd killed Delaney and was threatening Feldspar. He also was after some waitress he thought could'a overheard him and Angel talking at the club. Angel was panicked. Said he hadn't planned on being tied into no killings. He was shit-faced scared."

"Juggernaut was only supposed be the bag man. What the hell is all this about killing Delaney?" Frank mumbled under his breath.

"Do you know who Juggernaut is? What he looks like?"

"Naw," Bobby said, "he's some cold-blooded bastard outa L.A. I never saw him."

Bobby paused then said, "Angel wasn't no threat. Hell, he wasn't Einstein, but he did his job and kept his mouth shut. Now he's dead. Shit, now I gotta go see his wife and kids. Man, what a pile of crap this is."

"Listen, Bobby, there has to be some other contact, someone pulling the strings."

Frank waited through the silence on Bobby's end of the phone. Bobby wasn't talking. Frank pushed harder.

"Bobby, Angel was a decent guy, a little stupid maybe, but basically decent. Like you said, this Juggernaut SOB killed him in cold blood, killed Delaney, and may have already killed some innocent girl. No telling how many others he's killed or plans to kill. Angel's family could be next. Hell, *you* could be next on his list!"

Galpino hesitated. He retraced his steps, trying to think it through.

Barkley was the only one he'd told about Angel's phone call and Juggernaut's plan to kill the waitress. Barkley had been his partner in the original scheme to bribe the councilmen for votes. Barkley had convinced Bobby that by combining their resources, they'd have big money to entice the votes their way. For Bobby, it was to keep zoning ordinances at status quo and to repeal the no-touch laws. For Barkley, it was some big land deal.

But it was Barkley who put Juggernaut on line as the bagman. It was Barkley that brought in Stella to organize the parties and Vegas trips for the councilmen.

Now it was all falling into place for Bobby, Delaney's death, then Stella's, and now Angel's. Barkley was eliminating anyone and everyone connecting him to bribes. Once his deal was OK'd, he would cut the connection to Bobby too. The way Galpino saw it, Barkley was reneging on their agreement and setting Bobby up for the hard fall, maybe even setting him up to take the hit for the killings.

Bobby Galpino saw Barkley in a new light. For Bobby, it was an epiphany on a grand scale.

"He's a cockroach, Frank. The man's a *fucking* cockroach!" Bobby hissed.

"Bobby, it's about damage control now. I gotta know who he is to be able to do something!"

"Barkley," Bobby said. "You get that *sonofabitch* Jarvis Barkley!" Then he hung up.

CHAPTER 61

Frank ran the scenario in his head. He and Willis had been on Bobby Galpino's trail for some time.

They had managed to convince a federal judge of the corruption scheme and had placed several bugs on councilmen's phones in hopes of pinning the tail on the big one. They waited and watched. As soon as zoning ordinances landed on the city council docket, they figured they'd close in. But that was mysteriously held off, and they couldn't figure out why.

Frank nuked instant coffee and stood at his sink looking out over Friar's Road from his condo. The brew was vile, but he trusted the double caffeine-whammy to sharpen the edge on his thought processes.

Jarvis Barkley is one of the biggest land developers in San Diego. He's built more condos and strip malls in high-density housing developments than anyone in recent history. If Barkley was the top guy, then he must have had some major interest to drive him to link up with Galpino and the strip clubs.

Frank lined up the recent deaths starting with Angel's and working backwards. When he reached Stella Morris, the knot forming in his stomach tightened.

Shit! Of course Stella was the key! She was right in the middle of it. Willis said Theo had Stella's journal and that makes Theo a prime target for Barkley and Juggernaut, if they know. That's not such a big if!

When it hit him, Frank nearly spat his last swallow into the sink.

Shit! Theo said Stella's brother was in L.A. but was coming to town to get her stuff. "Oh, *jezzus!*" Frank said out loud. "It's all too pat. Oh, *goddamnit!* Don't let it be him!"

Frank dialed Theo's number. "Come on, come on, Theo! Pick up the damn phone!

It rang several times before the voice mail picked up.

"Theo, listen its Frank. You there? Pick up! Pick up the phone, Theo! This is an emergency! OK, listen, don't tell anyone about Stella's journal. I'm coming over."

CHAPTER 62

Theo felt like she was drifting and languidly floating during the ride down Laurel Street and onto Pacific Highway.

Familiar landmarks floated by like a virtual tour in a travelogue. She loved the soft pink colors of the neon edged Art Deco architecture of the *Fat City Restaurant.* Flanked by groupings of palm trees, each aglow with their own soft halo of golden light, it had always seemed to Theo like San Diego's imitation of a tropical paradise.

When they turned onto Harbor Drive, the historic sailing ship the *Star of India* loomed before her, full sails billowing in the salty breeze. They drove past, and she muttered that it was a lovely morning for a sail.

"That's where we're going, Theo," said Jack.

"We're going to take a little boat ride. How does that sound?"

Theo thought it sounded wonderful.

At the Marriott Hotel Marina, Jack helped her out of the truck. He waved to the security guard and yelled something about his girlfriend having celebrated just a little too much. The guard waved them on and continued on his rounds.

CHAPTER 63

Frank got to Theo's place just as Oren and Guy were getting into Guy's sporty Lexus SC.

"Hi, Frank," Oren yelled and waved.

"Oren, Guy, have you seen Theo? She doesn't answer her phone. She's not home."

Frank was clearly frantic. Oren knew something was wrong.

"She left with Stella's brother just now. You just missed them. I waved, being the hospitable guy that I am, but she just ignored me. Actually, she looked like she was drunk."

"What were they in?"

"Oh, it was one of those macho-bruiser trucks," Oren said. "A Ford F-250. Sleek black."

"Which way were they headed?"

"I'm pretty sure he turned left onto Goldfinch, toward town," Guy said.

"Thanks!" Frank shouted as he jumped back into his car and sped off.

Frank dialed Bobby Galpino and prayed he'd answer. Bobby picked up on the first ring.

"Yeah!"

"Bobby, its Frank. Listen, I'm just trying to stop this killer. He's taken off with a woman – a friend of mine. Do you have any idea where he'd take her?

"That sonofabitch has access to my damned yacht."

"Where?"

"Sheraton Marina. It's the *Pair-A-Dice.*"

"OK, thanks."

"No! Wait!" Bobby said. "I moved it. It's at the Marriott Hotel Marina, near Seaport Village."

Frank reached the marina just as the *Pair-A-Dice* pulled away from the dock. Frank jumped from his car and dashed toward the next docking ramp, and as the boat slid by, he leapt. Landing hard on the rear deck, Frank tucked and rolled, then found cover behind an elevated hatch.

He watched from the shadows as Jack Morris guided the boat through the harbor, past the hotels. The yacht slid past the runways and hangars at the North Island Naval Air Station, then past the Navy piers. Edging toward the tip of Point Loma, they passed Fort Rosecrans National Cemetery with its endless rows of white tombstones catching the early morning rays.

The sleek craft continued on to make its way through the harbor, passing the lofty Cabrillo National Monument with its landmark statue of Juan Rodriguez Cabrillo, gazing over the harbor he discovered.

Departing the mouth of San Diego Bay, they rounded the final landmark to the east, a rock pile on the southern tip of Zuniga Point Jetty. When they glided past the point, they were out of the channel.

Ahead lay nothing but the wide-open Pacific Ocean.

CHAPTER 64

Frank crept along the side of the deck until he reached the hold. He slipped down the stairs and found himself in the ship's galley. He reached for his cell phone hoping to relay the boat's location in time for the Coast Guard to board her before she made it to the open water. It was then that he discovered the casing was crushed.

Shit! Must have happened when I landed and rolled over. No cell and no gun. Perfect!

He grabbed a knife from the galley drawer and made his way back toward the cabins.

*   *   *

The drone of the boat's engine seemed to vibrate the bunk on which she lay. The steady hum pulsated inside her head like a chorus of tiny drums. Theo reached up to put some pressure against her forehead and that's when she realized that her hands were cinched in a plastic restraint, as were her feet.

She tried to piece together the chain of events that led from the sensation of euphoric pleasure she had with Jack to her current state, but the images were hazy. She vaguely remembered them talking about Stella's journal. Then, it all blurred into memories of warm caresses and whisperings. There was no link between that enraptured state she felt with him and where she was now. It wasn't a stretch for her to figure out that she had been drugged. But why he did it was the mystery. Theo wished she could just blink her eyes and wake up.

The pain in her head was ebbing to a dull ache. *This is no dream – this is real!* She was able to wrap her mind around that concept about the same time she was able to focus on her surroundings.

It was dark in the cabin, but she was able to make out wood paneled walls with louvered shutters on what must have been the cupboards. Theo raised herself and felt dizzyingly unsteady. She waited for the nausea to subside, then she tried to stand on her tethered feet.

Balancing was difficult, but she managed to hobble to the porthole opposite the bunk. She peered out, but couldn't tell where the sky and sea separated; both looked black and leaden.

Just then, the door of the cabin creaked opened. Theo braced herself against the side of the bunk as a man's deck shoes moved slowly down the steps. He called her name. The voice wasn't Jack's. It was Frank's.

"Theo?" He whispered, again.

Then, he saw her propped against the bulwark, clutching the side of the bunk.

"Thank God, you're all right," Frank said, relieved.

He moved toward her and reached out his hand as if to touch her face. She shrunk back. The look on her face was enough to stop him.

"Look," he began. "I know you don't understand what's going on here. You've got to trust me. I'm here to help you. Believe me, Theo. Please believe me."

"Where's Jack?" Theo said thickly.

"He's up on the deck," Frank said.

"He's a dangerous man. He's . . . ."

The sound of the engines stopping brought him up short. He looked upward, then pulled a long shiny object from his pocket. Theo stiffened and pulled back as Frank came toward her with a knife.

He dropped down and snapped the blade through the plastic restraint on her ankles, then cut the one on her wrists.

"I've got to stop him before we get too far out into open water," Frank whispered.

He motioned for her to be quiet and to stay below then he bounded up the steps and was gone.

CHAPTER 65

For once, Theo actually considered following orders, but the reality of the danger they were both in overrode Frank's directive.

She crept through the galley and waited at the bottom of the stairs. She didn't have to wait long.

Soon, the sounds of a struggle on deck sent her looking around for a weapon. She found a small paring knife. She grabbed it slid it into her pocket, blade first. Theo steadied herself on the railing and crept up the steps and out on the deck.

The two men were wrestling in the shadow of the wheelhouse, their faces obscured. There was a sickening thud as one cracked the other's head against a metal pulley. He stopped struggling and became limp.

Theo shrunk back behind the cover of the cabin's door and watched as Jack raised himself off Frank, who was now spread-eagle and unconscious.

Jack ducked into the captain's deck wheel room, then he reappeared with a revolver. He walked over to Frank, nudged him with his foot, then pointed the gun at his chest; he cocked the gun and was ready to fire.

"*Stop!*" Theo shrieked.

Jack wheeled around and pointed the gun at her and motioned for her to come closer.

"Over here, Theo," he said quietly.

Jack was smiling and talking in a low soft voice.

"You should really let me shoot him, you know. I'm not really in to threesomes, at least not with two men in the picture."

Theo tried to conceal her terror behind a cool façade. She hoped she could catch him off guard. She hoped Frank would come to and pull a gun. She hoped for a miracle.

"Oh, I dunno, Jack," she forced a smile and edged closer.

"Seems like you might have better things to do with your time. Killing is such a waste."

"Some killing is definitely a waste. I'm going to hate losing you." He was smiling, but his eyes were cold and hard.

"You don't have to, you know. I could be of use to you. I think we proved that at my place, remember?"

He smiled, but didn't budge. She inched forward.

"I don't need scotch or drugs to show my affection."

She was smiling and continued toward him.

"I can be pretty accommodating when I'm fully awake."

"It's a pity I won't be able to take you up on your offer, Theo. I did feel a real connection with you from our first meeting. Too bad you had to meddle. You know too much. And in your case, too much information is a fatal flaw. Very fatal."

Theo tried to keep Jack distracted. Frank's life depended on it.

"You're not really Stella's brother, are you, Jack?"

He laughed.

"Would it make a difference to you?"

"It would make some sense out of all this."

"Actually, I am," he corrected himself, "*was*, her stepbrother. Yes, we had a lot of quality time together, Stella and me, something that you and I won't have I'm afraid."

"She talked about Juggie in her journal. Seemed like they were lovers? Is that you, Jack? Are you Juggie?"

"Do you know why she called me Juggie? No, of course not. How could you. Although, I was hoping to show you, pity that's not to be. Guess I'll just have to tell you."

"I'll bet I can guess why?" Theo crooned, licking her lips. She was trying to look nonchalant or seductive. She hoped she could stop their trembling.

"I've got one of the biggest in the business." Jack's smile curled at the ends of his mouth.

"That would be the porn business?"

Jack laughed outright. "Not sure I'd call it a *business*. For me it was all pleasure!"

"Is that what you and Stella did?" Theo continued, inching closer.

"Made good money too, at least it was good for a 19 year old stud and 15 year old school girl. We were hot – sizzling, actually!" He added, licking his lips.

Theo wanted to vomit, but managed to swallow the bile inching its way up the back of her throat. She continued forward until she was within arms length. That's when Jack reached out, grabbed her hair, and threw her against the railing. He rammed his body against hers, pinning her between his thighs and the boat's bulkhead. Then, seizing her wrists, he shoved her hands inside the waistband of her jeans, twisting it until she was tightly cinched, barely able to breathe and powerless to move.

With his other hand, he released his grip on her hair and slid the barrel of his gun down the line of her throat and across her breasts.

Theo gulped air struggling to breathe. Jack Morris laughed.

"Like it rough?" he whispered.

Theo felt the icy gun barrel beneath her breast.

"I do," he whispered, "and, sweetie, I can be very, *very*, rough."

Jack slid his tongue along her jaw, then across her lips, forcing them apart. He jabbed hard angry thrusts deep into her mouth. Somewhere between pure terror and fury, she found the strength to respond, hoping he would become aroused enough to weaken his hold on her. What happened next seemed like slow motion.

Jack eased his grip on her waistband as he groped for her zipper. He'd left just enough slack for her to maneuver her right hand. From inside her pants, she grasped the handle of the knife. Now he was fumbling with his own zipper. That's when Theo leaned in against his thigh and with every ounce of strength she could summon, shoved the tiny knife's blade through the fabric, driving it hilt-deep into his thigh.

Jack howled in pain, released his grip on her, and stumbled backward. He fired just as she dove sideways behind the wheelhouse.

By now, Frank had regained consciousness. He grabbed Jack's pant leg. Jack lost his footing and fell crashing down on top of Frank. They struggled in the shadows, and again, she couldn't tell one from the other. At that moment, the gun was wrenched from Jack's hand, and it slid just inches from the two struggling men.

Theo dashed forward and grabbed it. Instantly, the hairspring trigger discharged. The force of it propelled her backward onto the deck. For an awful moment neither man moved, then, from the darkness one of them emerged.

Theo raised the gun and pointed it with dead-eye accuracy as Jack lunged at her. The bullet struck him just above his left eye. His look of surprise melted as he dropped to his knees, then slammed, face forward onto the deck.

Theo scrambled over to Frank. Blood was pulsing from his shoulder, but he was alive. She was shaking violently and gulping in air when she heard it.

At that moment, she could have sworn that the whooshing thump-thump sounded like a giant angel's wings. Cradling Frank's head in her arms, the sound of her sobs were drowned out by the roar of the Coast Guard helicopter drawing in overhead.

CHAPTER 66

Waiting at hospitals was becoming a habit for Theo – one she decided she needed to break.

The doctor said it was a miracle the ricocheted bullet only ripped out a thumbnail-size chunk of soft flesh from Frank's shoulder. It would be a painful reminder for a long time, he said.

"A few centimeters to the left and it would have severed an artery. Your man's damn lucky," the doctor added.

"Can I see him?" Theo asked.

"In a few minutes," the doctor replied, "we'll finish sewing him up and let you know when he's back in his room. But he'll need to sleep for awhile."

Theo nodded. Agent Willis gave Theo a reassuring look.

"That's too close for comfort! Frank's lucky you saved his life."

In the waiting room, Agent Willis filled in the blanks for Theo.

"Frank has been working undercover with us. Through his job as vice cop, he was connected to Angel Martinez and Bobby Galpino. Frank gained their trust and was able to pick up enough information for us to know something was going down at city hall."

"We had a wiretap on Delaney, Feldspar, and Thomas for eight weeks, but weren't getting much. We dubbed them the 'Three Amigos.'" He chuckled.

"But the *Amigos* were being careful. Before we could move, we needed hard evidence. We needed the proverbial 'smoking gun.' We were getting snippets of conversations that could have been incriminating. But when Delaney was killed, all their conversations suddenly got 'pristine,' so to speak."

"Did you know about Stella's connection?" Theo asked.

"We knew she was a party girl and involved with Bobby Galpino. When you told Frank about Stella and Delaney, then it started to fit together like a puzzle. But no one figured the puppeteer pulling all the strings was Jarvis Barkley.

Theo was stunned.

"*Barkley!*" Theo gasped. "What's Barkley got to do with this?"

"Barkley's plan was to get his big land deal through, but in order to do it he needed some dirt on the councilmen. He couldn't be assured of their votes without a little strong arm guiding them. With the strip club bribes, he had it."

Theo stared at him in amazement. She remembered her conversation with Barkley the night of the fundraising gala and how defensive he had been of redevelopment and staunch support of the laws of eminent domain. Now, she knew why. He had an ulterior motive, and it had nothing to do with community betterment.

"It was all for power and greed," Theo muttered.

Willis shrugged. "Those are pretty strong motives."

Theo nodded. "Yeah, the worst."

"And what about Jack Morris?" she asked, wincing at the thought of how easily she had been attracted to him. An uninvited memory of his mouth on hers and his clear blue eyes boring into her sent an icy shock up her spine. She dispelled it with an involuntary shudder.

Willis caught the slight reflex.

"You all right, Theo?" he asked softly.

She nodded an OK, and Willis continued.

"Barkley brought Morris in as the bagman and muscle. He shuffled the bribes between Barkley and Galpino to the councilmen."

Theo was letting it all sink in.

"Morris was a vicious killer and got what he deserved. But Barkley's the biggest crook of them all, and he's still out there!" Theo said angrily.

Willis looked at her, a long scrutinizing look. Then he said, "I can't say any more about Barkley right now. But he won't get away with a thing. Don't worry. We've got him in our sights, more to protect him from Bobby Galpino!" Willis chuckled softly.

Theo took a breath and nodded.

"So this scheme was what brought Stella to San Diego?" Theo asked.

Willis nodded. "She worked for some of Galpino's other interests in Vegas."

"Do you think she knew that Jack was a killer?" Theo asked.

"Doubt it. Close as we can figure, he pretty much worked out of L.A. They were together there years ago, but then she went to Vegas. Somewhere along the line, they split up, lover's spat or whatever."

"But he was her *stepbrother*, how could he . . . ," Theo said, her voice trailing off.

"Look, Theo, the whole affair is ugly and sordid. Stella had a pretty long rap sheet herself. She'd been working as a prostitute since she was 18 and maybe before. We only have a record on her back to 18. Maybe she was trying to go straight. But once in that business, it's hard to get out. She was making big money. You can't make that kind of money waiting tables."

"She loved Delaney," Theo added as if in Stella's defense.

"Yeah, apparently," Willis said. "Seems that was their downfall."

"That's the irony," Theo said. "They tried to do the right thing and that's when the worst possible thing happened to both of them."

Willis nodded and shrugged his shoulders in mute acceptance of the paradox.

"Yeah, seems like no good deed goes unpunished," he mumbled.

CHAPTER 67

"We suspect that it was Morris who forced your friend's car off the road." Willis said.

"What do you mean? I thought that was an accident! Why in god's name would he go after Abby?"

"Actually, it wasn't Abby he was after. It was Connie Tominsky."

"Connie?" Theo sputtered, "But, why?"

"Yeah, I didn't get that either. Frank figured it out. When he got the report about Abby's accident, he rushed to the hospital. He said he needed to be there with you, said you and Abby were like sisters. But by the time he heard the report and got over here, you'd left. Ms. Tominsky was still here, though. She was so rattled, she told him about a conversation she overheard at the *Lion's Lair* between Angel Martinez and a strange man. We now know that man was Morris."

Willis drained his Diet Coke then continued.

"Only problem was that Frank didn't put two and two together until he got the call from Bobby Galpino about Angel's murder. The rest, as they say, is history."

Theo looked away. Her throat was dry and scratchy like burnt toast. Then, she felt the sting of tears. She fished her used Kleenex out of her pant's pocket and blew her nose.

That's when she saw the blood – Jack's blood – caked down front of her jeans. Her hand flew to her mouth. She looked like she would pass out.

Willis touched her arm

"You OK?"

She managed a shaky nod. It was the aftershock taking hold. Theo felt like she had been doused in ice water. She was trembling, and her breath was coming in jagged spurts. Willis pulled off his jacket and draped it around her shoulders. The warmth connected. Then the tears started.

Willis left momentarily. He returned with a steaming hot cup of coffee. Finally, after a few moments, she found her voice.

"If only I had known sooner, maybe I could have done something to help. Instead, I nearly got Frank killed."

Agent Willis cleared his throat and said kindly, "I doubt it, Theo. How could you know? This scheme was a maze. It took us way too long to figure it out."

"So where does that leave us now?" she asked.

Willis's phone buzzed.

"Willis. Yeah? What station? All of 'em?" He chuckled.

Willis picked up the TV remote and switched on the local NBC affiliate, channel 7/39.

The screen showed FBI agents raiding the city council offices of Feldspar and Thomas who were being led into waiting cars by the agents. Willis turned up the volume.

"Earlier today," the newscaster said, "FBI agents raided the offices of City Councilmen Chuck Feldspar and Bradford Thomas. The officers carted out boxes of materials and several computers. Yes, that's Feldspar and Thomas being led out of the building and taken away in separate cars. City hall is in an uproar as stunned staffers watch what may turn out to be one of the biggest corruption scandals this city has seen in decades."

Willis turned off the TV.

"Well, Theo, you know the rest."

Willis's cell phone buzzed again, and this time he said he had to leave. He asked Theo if she would be OK. She shook her head yes.

*   *   *

Alone now, Theo walked over to the window that faced west, in the distance she could see the bay and the Pacific Ocean beyond Point Loma. The sunset was rich and golden and set it all afire with its glow.

Theo shivered as she thought about the fallout from the scandal. The weeks of copy that would fill the papers and the radio and TV news and talk shows. She thought about Dick Bateman, her old nemesis.

Bet he's salivating right now, she thought. *He'll chew on this one for weeks.*

For Theo, however, the story was more than juicy copy. It was like discovering that a beloved family member was a criminal and having that reminder splashed on the front pages and filling the airwaves for everyone to see and hear. It was an embarrassment, a shameful reminder of the whole sordid mess.

She remembered her conversation that night at Bailey's when Connie told her about the money from Angel for Feldspar's campaign. Abby had thought that schemes like this should be expected. Theo wondered if most people would think that too.

It shouldn't be business as usual. Theo thought. *A "wink and a nod" at corruption and sleaze defiles every one of us.*

The sun was slipping into the sea, staining it a deep blood red. Soon, the twilight would blanket the city, and its windows would sparkle like a million twinkle lights on a Christmas tree. It would be magical and enchanting – postcard perfect.

It's over, she thought. *Frank's alive. Abby'll be OK. The bad guys are behind bars – or soon will be. It's a crime drama's perfect ending.*

The deep crimson sea slid into night.

Watching the city's transformation felt like her millionth. At another place in time the beauty of it would have inspired her, lifted her spirits.

Theo felt that those days were gone now. The deep sadness that hung all around her twisted the picture-perfect view. She was lost, adrift. Gone was the trust.

CHAPTER 68

Theo was dozing in the chair opposite Frank's bed when her cell phone buzzed. She grabbed it and stepped out of the room.

"Hello?"

"You were right in the middle of this one, sweetheart!" Sam Morley was excited.

"Sam! What time is it?"

"Early. Oh, baby, this is one of the biggest scandals this city's seen in long time. It's hot! I've got an army of journalism students chomping at the bit to work on this. I'm putting you in charge. This is Pulitzer stuff, baby!"

"Listen, Sam, I'm a little bruised right now," she said. "Besides, the TV and radio stations are all over this. How many ways can you spell *corruption, greed, and murder?*"

"Look," Sam persisted, "you can write an angle on this that nobody has. You can put a face to the name of every person who got caught in the crossfire, and you can put a personality to that dead girl. She was more than just some opportunist who got killed. In the end, she tried to do the right thing. She deserves a decent epitaph. Her's is not just some dirty little murder. Hell! There are no dirty little murders! That's the story that needs to be told." Sam said it with conviction.

Theo didn't feel like she had the energy to rally. She wanted to put it all behind her. She wasn't interested in reliving any of it in the telling.

"Do you think anyone really cares? They all think its politics as usual," she countered.

"Look," Sam said gently, "don't go kicking yourself for being an idealist. The thing is that while most of us act blasé about it, deep down we hang on to trust and hope – it's what helps us survive. It's the glue that holds us all together."

"Sam, I can't. I don't have it in me. Not now, maybe never again."

"Uh-huh." He gave her a moment.

"You get to feel that way now, Theo. You've been through a war. You're a little shell shocked. Maybe you think you've lost all faith. And true, what happened might be a good argument against everything you believe in. You get to hunker down for a while."

"Thanks, Sam. I just need a few days. I'll call you tomorrow."

Theo waited for his usual brisk OK and hang up. But he was still there.

"Sam?"

"Most of us get dealt a set of principles – from our parents, religion, school, even *Superman*, it doesn't matter. Sometimes we ignore them when they get in the way of something we want – or *think* we want. But eventually, they stick. We start to accept them because at some time we get that they're what keeps us on track – kinda like that white line that divides the shoulder from the road. It's always there – in good weather or bad. We don't pay much attention to it when the sun is shining, but when it's foggy or raining, it's our lifeline. It can mean the difference between a safe trip and disaster. When the weather is at its worse is when we look for it most. Our lives depend on it."

Theo sniffled. "I feel like an idiot, Sam," she said in a choked voice. "I feel dirty and deluded and stupid. How's that mantra go? '*Stupid, stupid, stupid!*'"

"You weren't stupid, kiddo, just trusting. Trust is a value worth preserving. It's the difference between loyalty and betrayal. It's the pure heart. It's the 'right' in righteous. And like it or not, what's right is still *right*," Sam said softly. "Someone straying from the law doesn't change the nature of the law."

Theo was still quiet.

"Well, you get some rest. Only . . . ?"

"Yeah, Sam?"

"You know, Theo, you're the only one who can make this real for them. It's the human interest perspective. It just might make the difference next time between apathy and action. It's all in the telling, Theo. It's what we do."

Theo mumbled good-bye and snapped her cell phone shut.

She leaned her head against the window and stared without really seeing.

In her heart, Theo still believed in truth, justice, and honesty. But right now, tired and bruised and tarnished by it all, she felt like she was a long way from home.

She reached for a fresh *Kleenex* and noticed the *Time Magazine* she'd left open on the table. She'd been leafing through the pages, barely scanning an article on former President Ronald Reagan while Frank slept until she too dozed off. Just then, it caught her eye.

Reagan was pictured behind his desk in the Oval Office. The quote below the picture read, "I know in my heart that what is right will always eventually triumph, and there is purpose and worth to each and every life."

There is no ignoring the little jolt you can get from idealism taken straight up, she thought. She couldn't even smile at the irony; it felt more like an indictment.

Theo pressed her forehead against the cold window. She thought about the people down in the streets and in their homes across the city. How some were probably listening to the news on their car radios as she watched and how some would soon hear about it on the evening TV broadcasts before they switched to *Wheel of Fortune* or *ESPN*. Many would scan the morning's paper and talk about it among themselves, maybe. Some would be outraged, some would chalk it up to politics as usual.

She thought about those that would wallow in the scandal for a brief time, then move on in the way that life does – the way that it must. The cynics would feel vindicated; the quasi-optimistic, sullied. But no one would be untouched.

Yet gazing into the distance from her vantage several floors above the street, Theo marveled at how the panorama seemed untouched. She recalled a fragment perhaps reminiscent of Bob Dylan, "You can always go home again, just not all the way."

*   *   *

The city stretched before her now, clothed in its shimmering cloak of night, a neon red ribbon of taillights streaked west on Washington Avenue toward the bay. It was a picture-perfect postcard but Theo's tears blurred the view.

EPILOGUE

Tommy Silver looked relaxed, almost at peace.

The ambulance paramedic wheeled the gurney into the examination room.

"We got the call from Father Donovan down at the Brotherhood Mission. That's where we picked him up. Looks like he dumped on meth or some other shit."

The morgue assistant glanced at the paperwork on the clipboard and then at the man on the gurney.

"Seems like a waste of time and money to autopsy this guy. Rules are rules, though. Pretty expensive looking suit for some street scag."

"Yeah, doesn't even look secondhand."

"Well, he won't be needing it where he's going."

He checked the pockets for ID and pulled out a tattered card, it read: "In case of emergency contact The Brotherhood of Jesus Mission" with a phone number.

He slipped the card with the few coins he found into the plastic bag then started to remove Tommy Silver's new Armani suit.

*   *   *

It was nearly dawn when Frank awoke. Theo was dozing in the chair by his bed. He kept his head turned toward her and watched her between catnaps.

The day nurse who checked his vitals awakened them both. She asked him if he was comfortable and if he needed something for pain.

"Pain can be a good thing," he responded, "at least I know I'm still alive."

"Hmmm." The nurse smirked. "Well, let me know if you change your mind when the morphine wears off," she said over her shoulder, closing the door behind her.

"You must be better," Theo said, smiling softly. "At least you still have your smart ass attitude."

"My smart ass is intact – it's my pride that's wounded!"

"You're just pissed because I got the bad guy."

Frank looked at her for what seemed a long uncomfortable minute.

"He damn near got us both. I'll never forgive myself for that."

Theo got up and sat on the edge of the bed. She took his free hand in hers and raised it to her lips.

"You know he nearly killed Abby."

"Yeah, and next he was aiming for you. I'm not much of a protector." He winced.

"You need something for pain? Want me to call the nurse back?"

He smiled slightly, then said, "Call her anything you like, but we don't need her right now."

He reached his hand up and pulled her head toward him. When they kissed, it was long and warm. For them both, it had the comforting embrace of home after a long absence.

"I've missed you," she whispered.

"I've missed me too," he said softly.

"You're just loopy from the drugs," Theo said smiling, but aware that his hand felt strong and warm as he gently stroked the back of her neck.

"Maybe." Frank sighed. "And *maybe* not."

"We're a damn good team," Frank said, his fingers pressing slightly harder.

"I nearly got us both killed," Theo murmured, starting to choke up.

"I think you should make it up to me," he replied, the corner of his mouth starting to turn up in a slight smile.

"I could use some R & R at your expense."

She reached forward and gently touched the lock of dark hair that curled just above his left eyebrow. She smiled, thinking it made him look like *Superman*.

"You think you could get a few days off?" she murmured.

"Yeah," Frank said, his dark eyes locked on hers.

"You?"

"I'm freelance. I get lots of days off."

He cupped her face with his hand. She nuzzled into the caress.

"The Mexican Rivera is a great place for R & R." Frank smiled, running his thumb over her full lips.

"I'll pack my bags," Theo whispered.

"Leave your laptop at home," he said, pulling her toward his waiting lips.